"In front o

Tara's arm shot out, her nails digging into Tucker's flesh.

Tucker jerked his head around to see a semitruck heading straight toward them. His blood froze. It was going to run them off the road! Tucker glanced at Tara. Her eyes were closed and her lips were moving silently.

Tucker swerved back into his lane. The 18-wheeler did the same. They were in trouble. If he ran off the road into the ditch, they could be seriously injured. And they'd be sitting ducks. He had seconds to make a decision.

"Hang on!" he shouted and yanked the wheel to the left. As if anticipating their move, the driver jerked the cab toward them, clipping the police car and sending them into a spin.

Time jolted to a stop, as if he was back at the controls of his chopper. The blur of green trees, Scout's yip from his kennel, Tara's terrified scream, all converged into laser-sharp focus. As they plowed through a guardrail, everything in him hoped God had listened to Tara's prayers.

Gina Bell lives in beautiful South Carolina, just a short hop to the mountains or the beach, both places where God's presence is felt in a powerful way. When not writing suspenseful stories filled with happily-ever-afters, Gina loves spending time with her husband, kids and grandkids, and taking long walks with her own special canine, a greyhound named Sugar Sweet.

Books by Gina Bell

Love Inspired Suspense

Outrunning Danger

Visit the Author Profile page at LoveInspired.com.

OUTRUNNING DANGER

GINA BELL

LOVE INSPIRED SUSPENSE
INSPIRATIONAL ROMANCE

MIX
Paper | Supporting responsible forestry
FSC® C021394
www.fsc.org

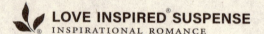

LOVE INSPIRED® SUSPENSE
INSPIRATIONAL ROMANCE

Recycling programs for this product may not exist in your area.

ISBN-13: 978-1-335-95756-6

Outrunning Danger

Love Inspired
22 Adelaide St. West, 41st Floor
Toronto, Ontario M5H 4E3, Canada
www.LoveInspired.com

HarperCollins Publishers
Macken House, 39/40 Mayor Street Upper,
Dublin 1, D01 C9W8, Ireland
www.HarperCollins.com

Printed in Lithuania

And let us not be weary in well doing:
for in due season we shall reap, if we faint not.
—*Galatians* 6:9

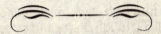

All the glory goes to God. He put this dream of writing on my heart a long time ago, and with unending whispers and nudges over the years, He never allowed me to give it up.

To my husband, Jack, my real-life hero, who read all my rough drafts and encouraged me every step of the way.

ONE

Tara Piper darted a final glance around the waiting room and flipped the sign in the window to Closed. Everything at Happy Tails Veterinary Clinic was in order and ready for business tomorrow morning. A sigh escaped her lips. It was a far cry from her previous life as a school guidance counselor, but she was getting used to her job here. And much to her surprise, she liked it, especially when the members of the Houston K9 unit brought their dogs in.

She just wished the office wasn't in a small town outside Houston, where she was staying hidden until she could testify in the arms trafficking case against Gideon Platt. Ivy, Texas, was too isolated and not at all what she was used to. She felt vulnerable and alone and wondered for the hundredth time why WITSEC placed her way out here. If she needed help, it would take a half hour for reinforcements to arrive.

This empty office was getting to her. She'd been living here for three months without a single incident. Fear hadn't consumed her yet. She refused to give in to it now, even though it had threatened to trample her like an angry bull every single moment since she'd agreed to testify in the case her brother had been involved in.

Tara had been so proud of Michael. She hadn't seen him

for years before the incident. He'd gone down a dark path, becoming an important player in an illegal gun smuggling operation. But then he'd come back into her life and told her he was trying to make things right. He had then become a police informant, working with an undercover officer to take down the corrupt organization from the inside.

For Tara, everything about the operation had been alarming. She knew being a police informant was dangerous, but her brother had always tried to play it down. He'd said he had a solid team around him who had his back, and she'd believed him, as if believing it was enough to make it true. But Platt's people had discovered Michael's betrayal and shot him. And Evan Schenk, Michael's police contact, and the rest of the team who were supposed to protect him had failed.

So, what had gone wrong? Fury burned in Tara's stomach. She knew what had happened. Her brother had been expendable. He took the risks. He got them the information they needed. Except they saw her brother as a criminal, trying to work the system to get out of jail time by giving them tidbits of information. And when it came down to protecting him when his cover was blown, they weren't willing to put their lives on the line. She'd learned from that experience that undercover cops were all the same, manipulating scenarios to fit their agenda. It didn't matter who got hurt.

Thinking about her brother brought her fingers to the dog tags dangling from a chain around her neck. They'd belonged to their father, and Michael had never taken them off. He used to joke about how the small metal tags tapping together when he walked annoyed him, so he'd encased them back-to-back in a plastic case for protection and for his sanity. Now that he was gone, Tara wore them. She felt as if a small part of her only sibling, and her father, were always close to her heart.

Tara paced from one side of the waiting room to the other. She remembered the day everything changed. Michael had begun to fear Platt was on to him, and in a moment of panic, he'd entrusted Tara with information about an organization that had as many arms as an octopus. Tara would have done anything to help Michael, but the facts he'd given her were what had landed her in WITSEC for the upcoming trial. If Platt ever found out what Tara knew about his smuggling operation, she'd need more than a single US marshal to protect her, no matter how capable her contact, Dan Cramer, was.

If ever there was a David versus Goliath situation, Tara knew this was it. Platt, a tech giant, was friends with CEOs, celebrities and politicians alike. He'd started his company, PlattTech Innovations, from the basement of his parents' home after he'd failed to qualify for the military because he was considered legally blind. Now, in an ironic twist, PTI often supplied cutting edge technology to the Department of Defense.

Tara had seen pictures of Gideon and he reminded her of a raven, with his black hair slicked back in a ponytail, and gray eyes that constantly shifted and darted behind thick, large-rimmed glasses. Looking for prey. The thought sent a shiver slithering down her spine. Tara wasn't going to let him get away with what he did to Michael. God would give her strength. She would get justice for her brother.

Tara stepped to the window and pushed two of the wooden slats apart. It was a straight shot to her car in the empty parking lot. A little scrap of paper danced across the asphalt, carried by a gust of wind as she craned her neck to look for shadows among the trees across the street and in the vacant lot next door. Unease brushed over her skin like a feather.

Dan Cramer had called first thing this morning and said he'd be there by the time she left work. She was needed at the US Marshal headquarters in Virginia. But why? The trial against Gideon Platt would be in New York. The sharp snap of anxiety hit her stomach. Dan hadn't given her any details, but tension had shredded his voice and had left her nerves in tatters.

Tara grabbed the car keys out of her backpack. No sign of Dan yet. She'd send a text and tell him to meet at her house instead.

Tara pulled the phone from her jeans pocket and blew out a breath. No signal. That had to be why she hadn't heard from him. Reception in this area was spotty at best. She chewed at her lip. Her little duplex was just a few miles away, and if Dan didn't find her here, he'd check for her there.

Tara pulled the door open, and her eyes flitted over the parking lot one last time for anything out of the ordinary. A hot breeze and the smell of baking asphalt greeted her, but otherwise it was the same unremarkable view she'd seen every other day since she'd been here. No shadows moved among the trees, no sinister figures peered around the side of her car.

Tara wasn't sure who she could trust since Platt's illegal empire was so vast, but she believed Dan was trying to help her. She squared her shoulders even though her mouth was as dry as cotton. Every instinct shouted something wasn't right.

With a click Tara pulled the door closed behind her and twisted the knob to confirm it was locked. A fly whizzed past her face, and she jumped and dropped her car keys.

She snatched them up and hesitated. The weirdest feeling someone was watching washed over her, and the hair on the back of her neck stood up. She stabbed the Unlock button on the key fob and the lock disengaged with a reassuring click. Tara dashed across the parking lot and then faltered. How had she forgotten to activate the clinic's security alarm? Frustrated, she turned and hurried back to the building and the world exploded.

Tara flew through the air and landed hard, as if a giant had picked her up and body-slammed her to the ground. The breath was expelled from her lungs, and pain ricocheted from head to toe. She fought to get air into lungs that felt like they'd been sealed shut, and clawed at the rough, dirty asphalt. *Get up, get up!* Glass and shrapnel rained down around her. A jagged piece of twisted blue metal glanced off her arm. She felt a sharp sting then the warmth of blood trickle down her skin. She had to get away. If she stayed here, she'd die.

With a grunt she pushed herself up on all fours and stumbled to her feet. Dark spots swam before her eyes, and the ground tilted. She tried to focus on the wreckage of her car, but it was a blur. "Please God, help me," she rasped as she stumbled back toward the brick building. A piece of rubber tire tangled with her feet and she pitched to the ground and lay there, cheek pressed against the hot pavement. The only thing she could hear was a rushing sound like a waterfall, muffled and distant, soothing in an odd way and lulling her to sleep. A wave of heat covered her and her eyes flew open.

Tara bolted upright and stumbled against the side of the building, crouching low and covering her head with her hands. A loud boom shook the ground, and a ball of fire engulfed what was left of her car. Bright red embers shot across the sky. One live cinder seared her cheek and she screamed, half crawling, half stumbling around the corner of the building. She leaned against the rough brick letting hot tears run down her cheeks and drip onto the front of her shirt. This couldn't be happening. But it was.

She rubbed her eyes, blinking against the dirt and grit that action brought with it. If someone was watching, they'd see their deathtrap didn't work. She was still alive. And she had to stay that way, because they were going to pay for her brother's death.

A tree limb that had fallen after the last storm lay nearby and she grabbed it, breaking the branches off. She'd played softball in high school and knew how to swing a bat. Tara took a deep breath, every muscle tense, and held the heavy limb steady in front of her. Over the ringing in her ears she heard the distinct sound of a twig crack behind her. Fear raced up her spine and she turned. All she saw were long blond hair and a baseball cap before a fist connected with the side of her head and she crumpled to the ground.

Tucker Dawson kept a tight grip on the steering wheel. WITSEC wanted Tara Piper picked up before she left work, and it had been a race from K9 headquarters in Houston to get there. All the chief had told him was that the location of her home was no longer secure and the US marshal's plane had been grounded.

Tucker had a description of her car and from a distance could see a vehicle in the lot that matched it, but something was wrong. It was sitting at an odd angle. As his brain began to connect the dots, a bright flash of light blinded him and his heart stopped. Her car had just burst into flames.

Tucker radioed a quick message to fellow K9 Officer Cade Pritchard requesting back up and emergency vehicles, and slammed the gas pedal to the floor. This was bad.

"Hang on buddy," he shouted to his partner Scout, a German shepherd dog trained in protection and suspect apprehension. Scout was safely secured in his specialized kennel in the back seat, but Tucker knew this turn was going to be on two wheels.

Gravel flew as he swerved into the lot and slid to a stop. His gun was in his hand, and he was out the door before the dust cleared. He stabbed at the remote attached to his belt and the back door opened. Scout leaped out, eyes bright and intense, ready for a command.

Tucker hurried to the clinic entrance, slowing as he passed the burning car. He twisted the knob, but the door wouldn't budge. "Open up! Police," he shouted, and pounded on the metal door. Everything was quiet and he cocked his head to the side, straining to hear any sound coming from within. The only noise was the sharp snap of the fire as it finished devouring Tara's car.

Several quick barks erupted from Scout, and Tucker spun around. The dog stood rigid, his attention focused on the corner of the building. Tucker nodded, then lifted his palm and motioned for Scout to stay. He moved along the building and paused, then jerked in a breath and pivoted around the corner, leading with his gun. A man with long hair was heading for the trees behind the clinic, a woman slung over his shoulder.

"Halt! Police," Tucker shouted. The assailant flung his arm back and fired a shot that went wide. He tripped, unbalanced by the weight of the woman he was struggling to carry, and threw her to the ground, stumbling onto all fours and then clawing to stand. Tucker flung himself at the assailant and landed hard on top of him. The attacker's head bounced hard against the ground. He stopped struggling and Tucker grabbed his handcuffs and pinned the man's hands behind his back. He hurried to check on the woman. It had to be Tara, but she hadn't stirred yet.

"Tara!" He rushed forward and crouched next to her. Her chest rose and fell in a shallow rhythm, and relief surged through him. She was still breathing. Long brown hair covered her face, and he pushed the soft strands back, his jaw clenching at the sight of broken skin and blood on the side of her head. There were numerous cuts and scrapes on her arms and face, and a splotchy red burn on her cheek. Tucker holstered his gun, then grabbed her wrist to check her pulse. It was steady and strong under his fingers, and he released a breath he hadn't realized he was holding.

He suspected this head injury didn't happen when the car exploded. Anger flared through him. The attacker must have ambushed her and hit her with a blunt object. His arrival had stopped him, but that meant another assailant could be lurking nearby. Tucker doubted that man did all this on his own. A soft moan tumbled from Tara's lips and her eyelids fluttered. This was good. He needed to get her inside right away.

Tucker moved in close and gently shook her arm. "Tara—" Her green eyes widened and she yelped, lashing out and swinging at him. She grazed his chin with her fist before he could duck. He leaned away and she lifted her leg, kicking him hard in the side. Pain radiated into his midsection and he grunted. Tara fought like a prizefighter. He held up his hands, palms to her.

"It's okay, I'm not going to hurt you. We've met before. Do you remember? I'm Tucker Dawson with the Houston K9 unit. You helped my partner, Scout, when I brought him in for an injury to his paw." He glanced over his shoulder where Scout waited. "Scout, come." The dog trotted over so Tara could get a look at him. Her frightened eyes darted back and forth between him and his partner. Relief surged through him as her breathing began to slow and she nodded.

He smiled. "Okay, good. We have to get you inside. Can you stand?"

"I think so." She nodded, then grabbed at her head and whimpered.

Tucker reached for her. "Here, let me carry you."

"No," she croaked. "Let me try to do it. I just need some help getting to my feet."

His arms went around her and he pulled her up. She gritted her teeth, and her breath came in short gasps. "Let's go," she said, her voice a husky whisper. "The door's locked but the key's on the lanyard around my neck."

"Got it. Lean on me so you don't stumble."

She nodded and nestled into him. Tara was slender, but there was a solidness and strength of muscle under his hands. She'd almost been blown up and then knocked out by a punch to the head, but she insisted on walking. He respected her grit.

A crack of gunfire split the air, and bullets drilled into the building, inches above them. Pea-sized nuggets of brick flew in all directions, showering them, and Tara screamed. Tucker scooped her up in one quick movement and ran for cover behind his SUV, Scout at his heels.

"Stay here," he said, setting her on the ground. He grabbed his gun and peered around the vehicle. The shot had come from the woods across the street, and he scanned the dark green depths, searching for movement. A second gun blast sounded, and a bullet crashed into the taillight just inches from his face. Tucker flinched and dropped back behind the SUV.

It was time to scatter some shots and see what he hit. Tucker leaned out, firing several quick rounds in the direction of the gunfire, then withdrew, pressing himself against the car. There was no return fire and he peered over the top of the SUV, squinting into the trees. There…he saw it. A brief streak of blue. "Halt, police!" The shooter didn't break stride, crashing through the trees and running at top speed. Tucker glanced at his partner. "Scout, apprehend." Tucker raised his arm and pointed at the retreating figure. The dog raced off, a blur of black-and-tan fur.

He glanced at Tara. She was watching him intently, and fear had turned her eyes into green glass. Sirens sounded in the distance, and he sagged with relief. "Help is here. I radioed for reinforcements," he said, and she nodded. Tears trickled down her face and without warning pricked his heart. He remembered how kind she'd been to Scout when his partner was injured. She'd smiled with ease, even laughing at one of Tucker's jokes, and she'd stayed on his mind for several weeks after that, despite his efforts to push the memory aside.

The thump of feet pounding on pavement sounded behind him, and he glanced over his shoulder to see a medic rushing toward them. It was obvious Tara's cover was blown. The US Marshals Service would be relocating her, and he knew that meant he wouldn't see her again. Disappointment surged through him, and he shook his head in frustration. Where had that thought come from? After Rachel had betrayed him following his return from Iraq, Tucker had made a pact with himself. No emotional entanglements. Ever. It would be the best thing for Tara to leave. He would do his utmost to make sure she was safe until the marshals stepped in and took over, relieving him of a distraction he didn't need.

Her dark hair was tangled, and he lifted his hand and plucked a piece of ash from the top of her head. "I'm sure that's not the last of it," she murmured.

Tara looked like she needed a friend, and Tucker closed off all emotion as he took her hand and gave it a gentle pat. "I'll be back, but I have to get to Scout. He's chasing after the shooter and could need assistance." Her lips lifted into the tiniest smile, and warmth spread to his toes before he could stop it. He gave her fingers a gentle squeeze, then sprinted across the street and into the woods.

Scout would stay on the chase, but he had no way of knowing if his partner was okay and had been able to bring the shooter down. Unease hummed under his skin. Tucker stopped to examine the terrain, looking for trampled brush or broken tree limbs, and noticed a spot that looked like someone had plowed through in a hurry. Without warning the silence was shattered by the blast of gunfire, and Tucker's heart froze. Scout!

He thrust himself through the trees, slapping branches out of the way and dodging roots. The sudden, distinct sound of a motorcycle engine turning over reached his ears. There were several short revs before the motorcycle raced away, the sound of the engine fading in the distance. Tucker skidded to a stop and strained to hear his partner. All was still, and the silence lengthened, twisting his gut. The sound of something crashing through the trees reached him, and he grinned as a streak of dark fur burst through the shadows. Scout came to a stop, amber eyes raised expectantly for his next command. Tucker bent forward, hands on his knees, and caught his breath.

"Good job, boy." He rubbed the dog's head and glanced in the direction the shooter had disappeared. The assailant had gotten away and frustration tore at him. Tucker knew there were side roads that led to the highway and back to the vet clinic. If the perp was on the motorcycle, they'd hear him coming. But what if he circled back on foot? Tucker knew he had to be ready. He had to get Tara out of here.

TWO

Tara sat on a chair in one of Happy Tails exam rooms and fidgeted. The medic, whose name tag said Cody, asked her for the second time to be still while he finished cleaning and bandaging the gash on her arm. "I think this laceration will need stitches," he informed her. He began to dab at her various scrapes and scratches with antiseptic, and the constant sting made her eyes water.

"You also have a slight concussion and should get some rest," he instructed.

She shook her head and pain throbbed behind her eyes. "I don't think rest is going to happen anytime soon. Do you have anything for a crushing headache?" He gave her a stern look but placed a couple aspirin in her open palm.

A sharp rap sounded on the door before it was pushed open, and Tucker peered around the corner, Scout at his heels. Cody motioned him in and pointed to a small stool in the corner. Tucker eased his large frame onto it, balancing precariously as it wobbled.

He leaned back against the wall and drew in a deep breath. His hair was a mix of blond and brown down to his collar, and at the moment it looked like he'd been in a windstorm. When he'd brought Scout in for the injury to his paw, Tucker's hair had been pulled back off his face and his eyes had stood out like blue embers. He'd been kind and funny, and she decided regular law enforcement officers were different from cops who worked undercover and were trained to be deceptive and shady, just like the undercover cop Michael had reported to. It had thrown her into a spin.

"What?" Tucker asked. She blinked and he continued. "You're staring at me. Do I have twigs in my hair?"

He smiled, and she could feel the fire in her cheeks. "I wasn't staring," she said. His eyebrows reached his hairline. "Okay," she admitted. "I was. Why is your hair so long? I didn't think that was police regulation."

"I work undercover occasionally. Helps me blend in."

Acid hit her stomach. "I didn't realize you worked undercover."

He shrugged. "Sometimes. Does that bother you?"

"Yes…no. It's your job. It's not my concern." His forehead creased and she continued. "It's just that people in law enforcement keep so many secrets. You get innocent people to help you and don't give them all the facts."

Tucker leaned forward and propped his elbows on his knees. "I'm not following."

"Never mind." She dropped her gaze. "It's nothing. Anyway, Scout looks as good as new after that laceration to his paw."

She glanced back at Tucker, who was watching her with an odd expression on his face. "He's a beautiful dog," she added, with a nod in Scout's direction.

Tucker lifted his arm in an arcing motion and pointed toward Tara. Scout walked over and sat next to her. "He's not just my dog, he's my partner. And he's going to help me get you to a safe place."

Tara reached out and stroked the dog's thick fur, feeling some comfort in Scout's presence. She knew he wouldn't leave her side as long as Tucker commanded him to stay, but as ridiculous as it seemed, the softness in his eyes gave her the feeling he wanted to be there. She shook her head. Was she really getting mushy about a dog? Cody must be right—she did have a head injury.

Tucker stood and walked to the window, his head moving as he surveyed the area outside the building. His cheeks puffed and he expelled a blast of air. The handsome officer seemed eager to get moving, and she couldn't agree more. Platt's thugs knew she was here. She had to disappear…again.

The exam room door opened and another officer stepped in, his head almost grazing the top of the doorframe. Trotting next to him was a bright-eyed beagle. Other than a short tail wag at the sight of the other dog, Scout didn't move. The officer motioned Tucker over and Tara tilted her head to try and hear the conversation. It had to be about her because the new officer kept glancing at her while speaking. Each glance ratcheted her blood pressure up another notch.

"Tara, this is Officer Cade Pritchard and his partner, Shiloh," Tucker said as they approached. "She's trained to sniff out explosives."

The rangy officer glanced down at the beagle. "Shiloh and I did a search of the building and perimeter, and there's no evidence of any other explosive devices. The only one was in your vehicle. It appears the bomb was set to go off when you unlocked the car door."

Tara felt the room spin as Cade's face blurred.

"Tara, what is it?" Tucker knelt down, his eyes roaming over her face.

"After I unlocked the car, I remembered I'd forgotten to punch in the code for the alarm, so I turned back toward the building. If I hadn't—" A shudder rattled her entire body.

He grasped both her hands in his. "It was a close call, but you're fine now."

"I guess God's watching over me," she said on a shaky breath.

Tucker's lips crooked in a small smile that made his eyes crinkle, and her heart missed a beat. That unnerved her. Why did she care if a secretive, undercover cop had a nice smile? And no way should her heart flip-flop because of it. "Whatever the cause," he continued, "you're safe and we intend to keep you that way."

She cleared her throat and slid her hand out of his grasp. "So, what now? Where am I supposed to go?"

Tucker rose to his feet, flicking a quick glance at Cade. "You're coming with Scout and me," he said. "I have orders to take you to our office in Houston, and from there a US marshal will meet us to transfer you to a safe location."

Tara jumped up and paced to the other side of the room. "How did they find me? What's to keep them from finding me again? That's the obvious place to look for me, at the police station." Her eyebrows drew together. "What are you not telling me?"

Tucker rubbed his hand across the back of his neck. "We don't know for sure yet how they found you. But you can't stay here. Whoever is behind this knows the car bomb didn't work—you're still alive. And the shooter Scout was chasing managed to get away. Right now, the only safe place is the police station."

Tara crossed her arms over the sudden chill that went bone-deep. What choice did she have? She couldn't go back to her home. If they knew where she worked, they had to know where she lived. She would have to start over. If they didn't find her first.

Her gaze locked on Tucker, and her heart thumped. The

warmth in his eyes made her blood zing. But she could never trust him, or anyone in law enforcement. She was afraid to. They used people and covered up facts for their own ends. Why would Tucker Dawson be any different? Her brother would still be alive if he hadn't trusted an undercover cop. Tara was not going to make that same mistake.

Grief surged in a rush that threatened to choke her. She knew the Bible said to forgive, but all she could focus on was justice for Michael. She had to stay alive long enough to see Gideon Platt and his empire of gun smugglers and thugs pay for her brother's death. She would be there to testify.

Tara nodded at Tucker, who released the breath he'd been holding. She would go with him because she had no other choice. She would do it for Michael. But she would watch Tucker Dawson like a hawk.

Tucker frowned. His gut told him something wasn't adding up. He understood Tara's fear, but it seemed as if she didn't want their help and that made no sense. They were the good guys. Right now, he and his K9 unit were the only ones standing between her and whoever was trying to kill her.

She must have valuable information on someone, but he and his unit hadn't been briefed on what it was. He knew all about the rules in the US Marshals Service, the priority to keep details private for people in WITSEC. Still, it didn't sit well. During his time in the army as a helicopter pilot, if he hadn't been kept in the dark during what he thought was a routine mission in Iraq, an army ranger wouldn't have been killed.

Images flashed in his head, and he swallowed back the guilt that clawed its way out of his stomach like a wolverine. Nausea made his hands slick with sweat, and his heart pounded. He stood and walked to the window, sucking in deep breaths until his pulse returned to normal. He'd come so far, but there were triggers that took him right back to the scene. When he'd cried out for the Lord to save Deacon, He hadn't. Where had God been on that day?

Tucker shook his head. That was for another time. His priority had to be on Tara and getting her back to headquarters so the US Marshals Service could get her to a safe location.

He turned to Scout, who remained next to Tara but kept his attention focused on his partner. "Scout, stay. Protect."

Tara tilted her head and stared at him until his skin began to prickle. He suspected she saw more than he wanted her to. He sighed in relief when she turned back to his partner and smiled. She might resent Tucker's presence, but she seemed to have a soft spot for Scout. For now, Tucker would take what he could get.

His phone buzzed and Tucker glanced at the screen. *Marcus Seever.* He motioned at Cade to follow him outside. "It's the chief," he said as he answered the call. "Tucker Dawson here."

"Tucker, Cade reported Tara Piper survived a car bomb but was attacked outside the building." The chief hurried on without waiting for Tucker to respond and warning bells sounded in his brain. "Get her back here to headquarters ASAP. Deputy Marshal Dan Cramer was found this afternoon."

Tucker sucked in a breath. *Found?*

Marcus continued. "There were bullet holes in the windshield and his car had been run off the road. He's in surgery right now in critical condition."

Dread hit his stomach like a rock. "Sir, is there a leak?"

The chief sighed and Tucker could picture him running a hand over his bald head. "Our contact at the US Marshals' office thinks so. I'm sending additional reinforcements to meet up with you and escort you back."

Tucker's blood turned to ice. The ramifications of a leak in the US Marshals' office were staggering. The focus seemed to be on Tara, but what about other witnesses? "She's just finishing up with the EMTs. What's the plan when we get to headquarters?"

"I'm working on it," Marcus responded and disconnected the call.

Tucker pocketed his phone. This situation had just gotten a lot more complicated and dangerous.

"What's with the scowl, Tucker? What's going on?" Cade asked.

Tucker glanced at Cade. "The plan is still the same. Get Tara back to our HK9 office. But the logistics have changed. Whoever's behind this car bomb attacked the deputy marshal."

Cade's dark eyes narrowed. "There's a leak?"

"We can discuss that later. We've got to get out of here… now." Tucker scanned their surroundings. The fact that nothing moved among the trees didn't ease his concerns. It was a half hour drive back to headquarters, and they were going to be as vulnerable as lambs until they rendezvoused with additional law enforcement.

"I'll take Tara in the lead. Cade, you and Shiloh bring up the rear. Keep your radio on and alert me if you see anything the least bit suspicious," Tucker instructed, already moving toward the building.

Tara jumped as Tucker bolted into the exam room and Scout sprang up, ready for action. "We're heading back to headquarters now," he said. "You'll be riding with Scout and me."

Tara's green eyes clouded. "What's wrong?"

"The chief wants you back at our unit headquarters right away, so we're moving out." He held his hand out to her and she stared at it, then moved to stand in front of him, so close he could see a small scar hidden in her left eyebrow.

"What are you keeping from me?" she said, her breath brushing against his face.

Tucker hesitated. How much should he tell her? She was frightened, and he wasn't sure she trusted him. Would finding out Dan had been attacked push her over the edge? He thought about the strength she'd already displayed and decided she wasn't the kind to fall apart.

"It's about Deputy Marshal Dan Cramer." She stiffened and bit her lips together. "He was ambushed. He's still alive, but he's in surgery. Chief Seever wants you back at our headquarters right away, for your safety."

Without a word she nodded and rushed past him. He followed closely as she hurried across the parking lot, her steps faltering as she glanced at the smoking wreck of the car. He could see the wetness on her face before Tara swiped at it with the back of her hand. Her life had been flipped upside down once again, and without permission his heart ached for her.

Tara climbed in and pulled her seat belt on while Tucker made sure Scout was secure in his kennel in the back. He gave Cade a thumbs-up and got behind the wheel. Adrenaline elevated every sense, and he scanned the area one last time before turning onto the highway. In his rearview mirror he saw Cade's vehicle exit the parking lot and keep pace about two hundred feet back.

Tucker glanced over at Tara. She clasped her fingers together in her lap and whispered softly. "Jesus, You go before us, behind us and around us. Thank You for Your divine protection." Her eyes locked on his for a beat, then she turned to stare out the window. The silence lengthened until Cade's voice crackled. "There's an old pickup truck a good distance behind me. Pulled out at the last side street. I got a glimpse of the driver when I went past and the man had white hair, looked elderly. He's keeping pace with me but hasn't made a threatening move."

"Got it. I hope he's just a local," Tucker replied. "Update if anything changes."

He eyed the rearview mirror, catching a flash of the rickety pickup as the road curved. He darted a quick glance to the left and right. Trees and small houses zipped by but nothing to cause concern.

"Your fingers are going to cramp if you keep a death grip on that steering wheel," Tara remarked. "Are you nervous? That's not making me feel any better, you know."

Tucker flexed his fingers on the wheel and glanced her way. There was a slight smile on her lips, and he blinked at how pretty she was. When he'd brought Scout into Happy Tails, he had enjoyed their conversation. His gut told him she was kind and decent and didn't deserve this chaos.

He took a deep breath and rolled his shoulders up and down, forcing himself to relax. "I'm not nervous," he replied. "You're in good hands. It's just barely contained energy."

She chuckled, and his heart beat even faster. "You make it sound like you're a superhero or something."

He glanced at her and grinned. "There are no phone booths out here, so I couldn't change into my cape." Her eyes locked on his before she lowered her gaze and turned to stare out the window again.

"You know, you have God. You don't really need a superhero," she murmured.

He tapped his fingers on the steering wheel. "I think God picks and chooses who He helps."

She shook her head. "I don't think so. I've dealt with some pretty harsh things. I've never felt God abandoned me—"

"Tucker." Cade's voice filled the cabin of the vehicle. "That old pickup has moved in closer. No threatening moves but he's creeping up."

"Got it," Tucker responded. "Stay frosty. It may be nothing. Maybe grandpa has a lead foot," he joked, trying to ease the strain that covered Tara like a blanket. He glanced at his passenger, who gave him a weak smile. He'd take it.

"Tucker." Chief Seever's voice boomed over the radio. "Backup is on the way. Given your location, you should see them in about fifteen minutes."

"Thanks, Chief. So far so good, but they can't arrive soon enough."

"They'll escort you through the back entrance once you arrive at headquarters—"

"Tucker, I'm under attack!" Cade shouted through the radio. Tucker glanced in the rearview mirror long enough to see the rusty old truck weaving alongside Cade's vehicle, attempting to ram it from the side. The crack of gunfire sounded through the radio, and the SUV plowed off the road into the ditch. Tucker's heart stopped. He needed to turn around and check on Cade but that could be leading Tara right into a trap with the driver of the pickup. He glanced in the rearview mirror. There was no sign of Cade emerging from his vehicle.

"You can't just leave him back there!" Tara exclaimed.

"We have to." Sweat flashed over his body and his stomach rolled. Everything in him rebelled at leaving his fellow officer and friend behind. "My orders are to get you to headquarters. Cade's an excellent officer. He'll be fine until backup gets there." Tucker believed those words, but these were unpredictable circumstances. He couldn't let Tara know the extent of his concerns.

"Tucker, update." Marcus's voice sounded through the radio.

"The pickup truck behind Cade opened fire," Tucker reported, working to keep his voice neutral despite the acid churning in his stomach. "Cade's SUV went into a ditch. I lost sight of the pickup. Per orders, I'm continuing to headquarters with Ms. Piper."

A heavy sigh greeted them before the chief responded. "We have the location of his SUV. I'll notify the local police and have a chopper standing by. Keep going, don't stop for anything. Law enforcement should rendezvous soon." The chief disconnected.

"The cavalry's on the way," Tucker said with a glance in her direction. She nodded, her gaze lingering on his briefly before looking away. He'd make sure she got back in one piece.

Tara's arm shot out, her nails digging into his flesh. "In front of us!" she shrieked.

Tucker jerked his head around to see a semitruck about a half mile in the distance, heading straight toward them in their lane. His blood froze. There were no other approaching vehicles, so he jerked into the oncoming lane, sucking in a horrified breath as the truck mirrored his move. It was going to run them off the road! Tucker glanced at Tara. Her eyes were closed, and her lips were moving silently.

Tucker swerved back into his lane. The eighteen-wheeler did the same. They were in trouble. If he ran off the road into the ditch, they could be seriously injured. And they'd be sitting ducks. He had seconds to make a decision, and he hoped it was the right one. The truck barreled down on them and the massive grille filled the windshield, blinding in the slanting rays of the afternoon sun.

"Hang on!" he shouted, and yanked the wheel to the left. The SUV veered sharply back into the oncoming lane. As if anticipating their move, the driver jerked the cab toward them as the huge truck roared past, clipping the rear quarter panel of the police car and sending them into a spin.

Time jolted to a stop, as if he was back at the controls of his chopper and every second was life and death. The moment crystalized in his memory. The blur of green trees, Scout's yip from his kennel, Tara's terrified scream—all converged into laser-sharp focus. The steering wheel vibrated and jerked as they barreled off the highway and he tightened his grip, fighting for control of the vehicle as it moved with a mind of its own. Tucker didn't believe God paid attention to him, but as they plowed with a vengeance through a guardrail and crashed through brush and bushes, everything in him hoped God had listened to Tara's prayers.

THREE

The sky and trees blurred together as the SUV spun in stomach-churning circles. Tara's clutch tightened on Tucker's arm and she pushed back into her seat, bracing herself. She risked a brief glimpse at him. His face was a mask of concentration, and he had a white-knuckle grip on the wheel as he tried to control the vehicle. She squeezed her eyes shut. A startled bark erupted from the back seat. *Scout!*

The squeal of tires and the burning smell of rubber assaulted her as they swerved across the highway and bumped violently over the brush and ruts along the edge of the road. Branches screeched along the side of the vehicle as it skidded. With a jarring thud, the SUV tipped onto the passenger side and slid to a halt. Tara's side airbag deployed, and pain ricocheted down her neck and arm as her head jerked sideways. She felt groggy and dragged her eyes open. Had she passed out? Her head throbbed, and she thought she might be sick.

Strong fingers grabbed for her, and she gave a shocked scream. "Tara, it's me, Tucker. We have to get moving." She felt his weight as he leaned across and unfastened her seat belt. "Scout, speak," he commanded. The reassuring bark of the German shepherd filled the interior of the vehicle.

Tucker grabbed the key and maneuvered through the

opening to the back seat and into Scout's kennel, then reached for her as she crawled through the narrow passageway. Her head swam and she pitched forward into the opening. Tucker grabbed her and pulled her close. His arms tightened around her. "I've got you," he murmured. It felt safe in his embrace, and she allowed herself to stay there for just a moment before she remembered he was an undercover officer and pulled back. Tension tightened the edge of his jaw, and the eyes that scanned her face were intense.

"We're going to get out of here," he said. She nodded and Scout nudged her shoulder, seeming to echo his partner.

"The driver probably thinks we're incapacitated. I'm going to take him by surprise before he can get to us." His brow furrowed. "I wish I had an extra weapon. Do you know how to fire a gun?"

She nodded. "It's been a while though."

"Maybe it's just as well then," he said with a wink.

She opened her mouth to reply, but Tucker had already brushed past her. With a gentle nudge he cracked the door open and peered out. Tara half expected a bullet to come zipping through the narrow opening. Everything was eerily quiet. "Just wait here with Scout. I'll be right back." He rubbed the thick fur behind the dog's head. "Scout, protect."

Tucker pushed a button on the K9 remote and the door sprang open. With a grunt, he scrambled up, eyes darting to his left and right. He glanced back at her and their gazes locked and held for a moment, then he jumped over the side. Tara heard the thud of his feet hitting the ground and a rustle as he moved through the brush to the back of the vehicle.

The silence was heavy, and the sudden loss of Tucker's presence made her feel off-balance. She hadn't realized how comforting it had been to have him there. Tara frowned. There was no point in getting attached to Tucker Dawson.

He was an undercover officer. Not to be trusted. After a few short hours, she wouldn't see him again. The thought squeezed at her heart and she brushed it aside.

Tara crouched next to Scout and stared into the dog's golden-brown eyes. "We're going to get out of here," she whispered. "But I can't just sit here doing nothing." A quick glance around Scout's spacious kennel showed little to use as a weapon. She stuffed her hand into the pocket on the back of the seat and her fingers circled around something brick hard. It was a heavy red rubber dog toy. This could work. Tara stood up too fast, wobbling with pain that rocketed through her head and sent white lights dancing in front of her eyes. She grabbed at the back of the seat to steady herself, feeling disoriented from trying to stand up in a vehicle on its side.

A growl started low in Scout's throat, and panic shot through her like wildfire. "What is it, Scout?" she whispered, holding her breath and straining to hear anything. The screech of a bird sounded in the woods, but otherwise everything was quiet. Maybe the dog was imagining things. Then, as soft as a whisper it reached her ears—the slight brush of something against the side of the car.

Her heart hammered against her ribs. Scout sprang to his feet, his fur standing on end. Tara twisted to look up and a man with a bent nose and slits for eyes sneered at her over the top of the door. She opened her mouth to scream as his hand snaked into the car, grabbed her hair and yanked. She shrieked as another hand grabbed under her arm. Tara's mind struggled to grasp what was happening even as she was lifted up, feet dangling in the air. She could feel the edge of the door cutting into her back as the man struggled to pull her out of the car. She grasped at the frame, trying to hang on as he fought to get her over the side.

A thunderous bark erupted from the confines of the SUV, and Scout was a blur as he leaped up and tried to sink his teeth into the man's arm. The attacker cursed and jerked his arm away before Scout could get a hold of it and fell backward, pulling Tara with him. He landed hard on his back, his breath erupting in her face and sending a wave of nausea through her. The man's grip loosened for a fraction of a second and Tara rolled to twist off him, but his arm tightened around her neck and squeezed. Tara fought, clawing at his arm and kicking, trying to suck in oxygen. From somewhere a gun materialized in his hand. He was going to kill her. She couldn't give in. There would never be justice for Michael if she gave in. She fought harder, kicking and scratching, feeling dampness on the back of his hand where she'd drawn blood.

"Stop it," he growled. The pressure tightened around her neck. Her arms were lead weights and her vision began to blur. Blackness creeped around the edges, and she finally succumbed to the darkness.

Tucker held his gun in a tight grip and crept through the brush and grass, inching closer to the eighteen-wheeler. The truck was stopped along the side of the road, the massive engine idling. He hadn't seen the driver emerge from the cab. He must still be inside. Tucker circled around the semi, staying far enough away to avoid being seen in the driver's side mirrors. Anxiety surged through him. He didn't like leaving Tara alone for too long, even though Scout was with her. But if he could bring this perp in, they may be able to get valuable information from him that could help keep Tara safe. Like who had sent these thugs after her.

Tucker moved in closer, brambles tearing at his pants and scratching his arms. There was still nothing stirring around the truck. No flash of movement in the cab. Alarm bells started to ring. How could the driver have evaded him? His heart began to pound. He had to get back to his vehicle.

He turned, and the hair on the back of his neck rose. The unmistakable sensation someone was watching crawled over him. He darted for cover behind a tree and crouched, peering around the trunk, looking for any spot someone could be hiding. Waning sunlight filtered through the trees, casting shadows everywhere. Nothing moved. Above him he heard the rustle of a squirrel as it raced across the tree branches, but otherwise the only sound was the rumble of the semi.

Without warning something hard struck him across the back of the head. Lights flashed in his eyes and he stumbled forward, landing hard on his hands and knees. His gun flew from his grip into the tall grass. A flash of movement snaked through the brush, and the hard toe of a boot kicked searing blows against his side. Tucker grunted and rolled, grabbing his attacker's leg and yanking hard. The perp fell backward and landed with a thud.

Adrenaline spiked as Tucker pushed himself up and staggered back, scanning for a weapon. The assailant rolled over, reached into his jacket, and spun around. The afternoon sun gleamed along the sharp edge of a hunting knife clenched in his hand. The man wore a camo T-shirt covering muscles on muscles, and the gleam in his eyes was sinister and chilled Tucker's blood.

The goon lunged, the point of the knife aimed straight for Tucker's stomach. Tucker sprang to the side—he was more agile than the perp—and he'd use that to his advantage. The man lifted his arm and sliced the air, missing Tucker's cheek by inches. The K9 officer grabbed a limb off the ground and flung it at the man's head. He ducked, and Tucker sprinted in the direction his gun landed. His assailant cut him off, and his arm snaked out again, brandishing the knife. Tucker bolted to the side and grabbed the man's elbow, twisting it in a way it wasn't designed to move. The man cried out, dropped the knife and hunched on the ground, cradling his arm and moaning.

Tucker dove for the knife, then scanned the grass for his gun, spying it lying next to a broken bottle. He snatched it up and turned toward his SUV, then stopped midstride. The key. He ran to the semi, jerked the driver's door open and climbed inside, turning the engine off and pocketing the key. Over the sudden deafening stillness that followed, the unmistakable sound of Scout's urgent barking blasted through the air. *Tara!*

Whirling, Tucker broke into a sprint, skidding on gravel and leaping over brambles. He should never have left Tara alone.

The roar of a man yelling reached Tucker's ears, and he burst into the clearing next to his vehicle. About thirty feet away Scout was jerking his head back and forth, his sharp teeth attached like a vise to the assailant's arm. The man was flat on his back, his gun just out of reach. The attacker twisted, trying to wrench his arm out of Scout's grasp and keep a hold on Tara with his other arm tight around her neck. She hung limply, eyes closed and lips parted. *No, no, no!* He pointed his gun at the perp. "Police, let her go!" The man turned mean eyes on him and didn't yield an inch. Tucker advanced closer, aiming the barrel at the man's head. His lips twisted in anger, and he loosened his hold. Tara rolled off him onto the ground, unmoving. Sirens sounded in the distance, and the glow of red and blue lights shone through the trees. Finally!

"Get this beast off me," the assailant growled, trying to pull his arm out of Scout's jaws.

"He's fine where he is," Tucker said, moving forward to check on Tara. With his gun still aimed at the attacker, he cradled her with one arm and pulled her to a safe distance. He placed his fingers on her wrist, feeling for a pulse. It was faint but steady, and relief surged through him.

Officers from Houston PD and several EMT trucks pulled off the road next to them. "Scout, release," Tucker said as officers rushed over and surrounded the assailant. Scout let go of the man's arm and trotted over to Tara, giving her hand a gentle lick. Her eyes fluttered and she moaned as a couple of medics began checking her vitals. Tucker moved back so they could do their jobs but kept his eyes on her.

A police officer hurried over. "I'm glad to see you," Tucker said. "One of our K9 officers was run off the road about a mile back, and there's an injured man over at the semi. I need an officer and medic truck over there ASAP."

"Sir, here comes the K9 officer now," one of the medics shouted.

Tucker darted a look over his shoulder to see Cade's tall form weaving through the crowd of police officers, and he couldn't help but grin. Maybe Tara's prayers had worked after all.

One of the medics helped Tara sit up, and she rubbed tentative fingers over her throat. Tears rolled down the side of Tara's face. Anger thrummed under Tucker's skin, and he vowed he wouldn't stop until the person responsible for these attacks was behind bars. What had he been thinking, leaving her alone in the car? She could have been killed.

He squatted next to her and she turned to him, her eyes filled with fear and shock. With a gentle hand he brushed the hair off her face, tucking it behind her ear. "I'll be right back. I'm not going far." She gave him a thumbs-up before an EMT grabbed her arm and fastened a blood pressure cuff around it.

Tucker jogged over to Cade who limped toward him. Shiloh trotted at his side. "You're a sight for sore eyes!" Tucker exclaimed. "What happened?"

"I got a little banged up," Cade replied, glancing at his knee, "but Shiloh and I managed to get out of the SUV after it went in the ditch. The old guy in the pickup U-turned to check on the damage, and I fired at his windshield. He took off like a rocket. Shiloh and I hoofed it from there. I can't believe you took on a semi," he said with a shake of his head.

"These people who are after Tara mean business," Tucker said, frowning.

A medic approached, signaling Cade to follow her. "We need to check out that knee, sir. I saw you limping."

Cade shrugged. "I'm sure it's fine," he muttered.

"See you back at headquarters," Tucker said, giving Cade a brief nod and hurrying back to Tara. She was standing and talking with Stella McNair, one of his fellow K9 officers. When Tara saw him coming, she smiled, and against his will, warmth zipped through him.

"Glad to see you and Scout in one piece," Stella said as he approached. "I've just been speaking to Ms. Piper. She said she's never seen this guy before." She nodded her head toward the perp, who glowered at them from the back seat of the police car. "His name is Stuart Martin and he's your garden variety thug. Easy to hire and not real smart. I'll stay here while the police question him and see if we can find out whose payroll he's on." She glanced at the yellow Lab next to her. "Clove and I will sniff around that eighteen-wheeler, see what we can come up with."

He turned to Tara and found her staring at him. Even in the shadows of dusk he could see a soft pink creep into her cheeks as he closed the gap to stand next to her. "That's the last time I ride anywhere with you," she whispered hoarsely.

He grinned. "Hey, I thought it was a pretty smooth landing, for a superhero."

Her lips lifted at the corners, and his eyes locked on hers. He wanted to tell her they'd gotten the bad guys and everything would be fine. In his gut he knew it wouldn't. There was a leak in the US Marshals' office. Was it even safe for them to relocate her? She should remain in the K9 unit's protection.

Her smile began to fade. "There'll be more coming after me," she said, coughing and rubbing at the blotchy red skin of her throat. "If Platt knows where I am, it won't stop."

Tucker didn't flinch but his mind reeled. Gideon Platt had a huge empire. It had been in the news he was suspected of smuggling ghost guns into the US and Mexico. If Tara was involved with him, there were things she might never share. More secrets. He'd be walking blind. Just like before. Everything in his brain said to back out once they got to HK9 headquarters. Give this hot potato to someone else. What if something happened to Tara like it happened to Deacon?

Tara's soft voice brought him back to her side. "They killed my brother. They're selfish, murderous people." She bit at her lip and her wide eyes glistened. "I can't let it go. I have to live long enough to testify against him."

"You'll testify, I'll see to it." He nodded. "But I expect you to live a lot longer than that." Tucker grabbed her cold fingers and gave them a gentle squeeze. Her fight was now his fight. He kept his tone light, but inside he knew he had just made a promise he intended to keep.

FOUR

The refrigerator in the corner of the break room clunked as the ice maker loudly dropped cubes into the bin. Tara was relieved to have that small diversion. The only other sound in the room was her breathing.

She felt fortunate to be here in the K9 unit's break room instead of an interrogation room, which had been the chief's original plan until Tucker intervened. A criminal she was not, and she appreciated he didn't want her treated like one. Tara spared a glance at the turkey sandwich and chips on the plate in front of her and pushed it toward the center of the table. She hadn't eaten since breakfast and her stomach rumbled, but the thought of food made her queasy.

"You're going to need your strength. Try and take a few bites."

Tara jumped at the sound of the deep, warm voice. She hadn't heard Tucker come in. He walked around the table and dropped into a chair across from her. With a small smile he pushed the plate back to her.

She shrugged and picked up a chip, nibbling at it. The crunchy saltiness was delicious, and suddenly she was ravenous. She picked up the sandwich and took a big bite, then another. She glanced at Tucker and paused mid-chew. His grin was huge, and his eyes crinkled at the corners.

"What?" she mumbled over a mouth full of turkey sandwich. "You've never seen someone eat before?"

"Not with that much gusto," he chuckled.

"You said I have to keep my strength up," she said, wiping crumbs from her mouth and taking another bite.

"That you do," he said with a nod.

Something that looked like wariness flashed in his eyes, and she dropped the bread crusts on the plate and pushed it aside. "What's the plan now? When am I leaving?" Her full stomach did an uncomfortable flip-flop. She almost didn't want to know.

Tucker leaned his arms on the table and clasped his hands together. "The K9 team has a meeting in a few minutes. The chief is speaking with the US Marshals' office right now. I don't know what the plan is yet."

"Will you be coming with me?" The question flew out of her mouth before she could stop it. Her mind reeled. What did it matter if he came? She wasn't even sure she could trust him.

Tucker scratched his thumb over his forefinger and kept his eyes on the table. The seconds stretched and Tara swallowed at her unexpected tears. It was too much. The loss of Michael, the fear of living in hiding, having to testify against a monster like Platt. Is that why she'd come to depend on Tucker like this? Three hours ago, she hardly knew who he was.

She shifted in her seat. That wasn't true. She did remember the kind, smiling officer from when he'd brought Scout into the clinic—before she'd realized he was an undercover officer. But now she'd gotten a glimpse of the integrity and bravery behind the smile, and for the first time in months she was beginning to feel hope that someone had her back.

Tucker's lips quirked to the side. "I'm not sure, but if they assign a new deputy marshal to you, it's doubtful they'll include me."

Tara jumped up, nervous energy running like ants under her skin. "What about what I want? You're the one who got me here in one piece. And we had to dodge bullets and a massive truck to do it. Do I have a say in any of this?"

Tucker pushed his chair back and walked over to her. "Your safety is everyone's top priority." He rubbed a hand over the back of his neck and stared at the floor. When he lifted his eyes to her, they were shadowed with doubt. "I made a critical error when I left you in the SUV to track down the semi driver. It might be better for someone else to take over."

She grabbed his arm. His skin was warm underneath her palm, even through the material of his shirt. "You didn't make an error. You caught the semi driver who could have ambushed us while we were trying to fend off the guy who attacked me. Between you and Scout, you took care of both of them, and I'm alive to tell the chief about it. Which I'm going to do."

Tara ducked around him and moved to the door. Tucker caught up with her. "Tara, wait. Let's see what they say first."

Footsteps sounded in the hall, and Stella walked in with Clove following behind her. "Glad you're here safely, Tara."

"Yes," Tara nodded. Thanks to Tucker and all of you."

Stella gave her a warm smile, then turned to Tucker. "Marcus wants to meet with us. He just got off the phone with the US Marshals' office. I brought Clove to keep you company." Stella raised an arm and pointed to Tara and the dog walked over and planted herself next to Tara's feet. "She's good company and an excellent watchdog. You're safe with her."

Tucker turned to the female officer. "Tell the chief I'll be right there." Stella nodded as she turned and headed out the door.

Tucker planted himself in front of Tara and tipped her chin up until she met his gaze. Goose bumps skipped up her arms. "Stay here with Clove," he said. "I'll be back as soon as I can."

She stood motionless and listened as his footsteps receded down the hall. The silence felt more like emptiness, and she walked back to her chair and sat down. Clove huffed out a sigh and followed her, eyes bright and alert.

The memory of the blinding grille of the semitruck pounded in her head, and she whispered thanks to God that they survived. Little threads of guilt knotted in her stomach. She wasn't sure where she stood with God, one minute thanking Him for saving them, and the next angry that Michael was gone. But she knew He would never leave her. "Lord Jesus, even when things seem impossible, You show up in the midst of it. Your plan is better than any I could come up with. Keep us safe and give me the wisdom and peace to follow Your lead, even when I don't understand."

Tara reached down and stroked Clove's thick fur and wondered if God had purposely sent Tucker to protect her. An undercover officer. After everything Michael went through, she couldn't believe she felt safe with Tucker. After Michael's funeral, when undercover cop Evan Schenk tried to offer his condolences, Tara had told him to leave. Even through her grief she felt engulfed by waves of dislike for the covert officer her brother had spoken of so highly. She knew Michael had suspected Platt's organization was on to him. Had Evan tried to protect her brother? Michael's death was proof that he hadn't. They'd got the information they needed. Michael was expendable.

Tara wiped the tears from her eyes. "I will get justice for you, Michael," she whispered. As much as she didn't want to admit it, she was going to need help to do it. Her gut told her Tucker was a good guy, but her instincts had been wrong before.

Tucker marched down the hall, frustration zipping through him like an electric current. How had he been so foolish as to leave Tara in the SUV, even if she was with Scout? There were too many unknowns. Why hadn't he considered there might be two men in the semi? The thought that he might have returned to find that she'd been taken, or worse, made him feel like he was going to lose his lunch.

Chief Seever hadn't mentioned it, but Tucker knew him. He wouldn't allow too many lapses in judgment, especially when it came to a human life. And this one was under the protection of the US Marshals' office. Tucker stopped outside the conference room door and sucked in a lungful of air. Then another. If he hadn't stopped praying, maybe he could have asked God for help in this situation.

Tucker entered the room and familiar faces turned his way, some giving him a quick nod and others a smile. The Houston K9 unit was his family, and at this moment he was thankful every one of them would go to the mat for him.

Marcus glanced at him. "How's Ms. Piper?"

Tucker nodded but before he could reply, the chief hurried on. "I've just gotten off the phone with the US Marshals' office. Dan Cramer pulled through surgery. He's still in critical condition, but the outlook is good." There were several sighs of relief and the chief continued. "They're concerned about a leak and don't want to risk assigning a new marshal to Ms. Piper. They want us to get her to a safe location, somewhere off the grid."

Tucker's heart thudded. "Sir, I have a fishing shack on Galveston Bay. It's a pretty isolated place. It was a retreat for me after I got back from Iraq. The closest neighbor is about a mile and a half away."

Marcus nodded. "That could work—"

A sharp rap sounded on the door. When it opened, the vivid green eyes of the topic of their discussion peered around the corner. Tucker's pulse kicked up several notches as Tara entered, followed by Clove.

Marcus stood so fast his chair almost toppled. "Is everything alright?"

Tara nodded and shoved a section of hair behind her ear. Tucker tried to convey *what are you doing?* with his eyes, but it must have come out as a look of encouragement because her lips tilted up and she nodded, then turned to Marcus.

"Chief, I just wanted to let you know that Officer Dawson risked his life several times to get me back here in one piece. I feel safe with him." She darted a quick glance his way before turning back to Marcus. "I would like to continue having him and Scout provide protection for me. I believe my opinion should count for something in all of this since it's my life that's on the line here."

Tucker kept his gaze on the table but felt the weight of the eyes of everyone in the room land on him.

Marcus cleared his throat. "Ms. Piper, your safety is our number one concern. I've just spoken with the US Marshals' office, and we are going to continue being responsible for your safety until they're able to take over. We're finalizing some details, but to ease your mind, Officer Dawson will still be assigned to your protection detail."

"Thank you, Chief." Tara nodded. "Sorry for the interruption. I'll just take Clove and return to the break room."

She backed out the door, her eyes locking on Tucker's for a heartbeat before she closed it behind her.

Marcus turned to Tucker. A raised eyebrow wrinkled the skin of his forehead. Tucker had to bite his cheek to stop the grin that threatened. He told himself it had nothing to do with her spirit or how cute she'd looked peering around the door. He was thankful he would still be able to help her. It was personal to him now.

"We'll need a couple decoys to leave ahead of Tucker's vehicle." Marcus turned to Stella and Beckett, one of the unit's newest officers. "You two head out first. Stella, you in an unmarked vehicle. I want constant communication if either of you see anyone suspicious."

"You got it, Chief," Beckett replied, nodding.

"Tucker, there's an electric company van in the garage. The Houston PD keeps it for stakeouts, and we've got the use of it. We've secured a kennel in the back so Scout can travel safely. It doesn't have any bells and whistles, but I'm banking on the perps ignoring it in favor of our standard SUVs."

The chief continued. "Katie, I want you following the van. Keep a good distance so it's not obvious." The petite blonde officer nodded.

Marcus glanced at his smartwatch. "It's after midnight now. Let's meet back here in a few hours to finalize details and set departure for 7:00 a.m. There will be more traffic on the road then, and your vehicles won't be so isolated. Besides, three police vehicles and an electric company van leaving in the dead of night will draw unwanted attention." He glanced around the table. "Try and get a few hours of z's if you can."

The scraping sound of chairs sliding across linoleum reverberated around the room as officers stood and stretched.

"Tucker, a word please." Marcus nodded his head to a corner of the room, and Tucker followed.

The chief's bushy brows pulled together and his brown eyes looked serious. Little drops of anxiety hit Tucker's stomach. Was Marcus going to remove him from this case after all?

"You handled everything top-notch today, through several intense situations," he said. "Keep it up. Don't let your guard down for a second."

Tucker nodded, relief surging through him. "Thank you, sir. I've been kicking myself for leaving her alone to go look for the semi driver."

"Judgment call in the moment," Marcus replied. "You'd just avoided a head-on collision with an eighteen-wheeler. When Cade reported what happened, and what could have happened…" He shook his head. "Go get some rest. And tell Ms. Piper to do the same." A rare smile softened Marcus's features and Tucker nodded and left, eager to get back to Tara.

Tucker could hear voices before he even got to the break room. Stella had an arm wrapped around Tara and was leading her out the door. "I'm taking her to my office so she can get some sleep," the redheaded officer informed him.

"Stella told me we're leaving in the morning for a secret location. It sounds like a good plan." Tara nodded.

"It will work," Tucker assured her. "I'm the only one who knows about this place. And the key word is *rustic*," he said with a chuckle.

"Wonderful," Stella said, rolling her eyes. "As long as there's indoor plumbing."

Tara's laugh was husky and sweet, and warmth meandered through him. She gave him a wave as she and Stella linked arms together and walked down the hall. Tucker was dead serious about protecting her and keeping her safe. But something about her was rocking his world. She had a kind and gentle nature, but a strength that left him in awe. There would be no more errors. He had to stay focused on what he needed to do and keep any personal feelings out of it. He wanted the best for Tara, and between him and Scout, she would get through this alive. And his heart would remain locked up tight.

FIVE

Tara pulled her hair back, twisted it into a messy bun and secured it with an elastic band. Several tendrils sprang loose, and she sighed and shook her head. She'd had an hour of sleep. This was the best it was going to get. Her eyes darted among the officers who were going to help them get out of here safely. The tension was so thick she was surprised she couldn't see it like a mist floating through the air. She climbed into the van and pulled her seat belt on, then shifted her position as a spring in the seat threatened to push through into her backside. The older model van looked like it wouldn't make it to forty miles an hour, but Tucker assured her the Houston PD had made changes under the hood so it had some power.

Scout was secured in his kennel, and she turned to him and smiled. His amber eyes widened, then he lowered his head onto his paws and exhaled, eyelids drooping. The tension was not getting to him. She wished she could find that same state of peacefulness.

Tara turned her gaze out the window to where Tucker was getting some last-minute instructions from the chief. His hair was still wet from a shower and slicked back and secured with a hair tie. He was lethally handsome. *Good grief*, she thought, and shook her head to clear it. That was the last thing she should be noticing right now. She shifted in her seat, doing her best to dismiss the thought and focus on the gravity of her situation.

She hadn't been able to get a shower but was thankful she'd been able to trade her ash covered, dirty clothes for some clean ones. The jeans and T-shirt belonged to Stella and were a little large, but at least she didn't smell like a fire pit. Stella had put an extra change of clothes and a small bottle of shampoo in a bag for her to use when she got to the cabin, and her eyes misted at how kind and dedicated these officers were. It was like a family, and the weight of loneliness was heavy on her chest. With Michael's death, she had no more family.

Tara jumped as the back doors opened and Cade slid a box of supplies into the van. "Knowing Tucker, the only thing in the cabinets at that shack of his are an expired box of power bars and a couple cans of soup. Also expired." He chuckled. "You two travel safe. We'll be monitoring on this end."

"Thanks for your help, Cade," she said as the doors slammed shut.

The waiting had her nerves stretched to a snapping point, and Tara was eager to get started. She sighed with relief as Tucker climbed in behind the wheel, a baseball cap now perched on his head. He looked over, eyebrows lifted. "You ready?"

She nodded. "Where'd you get the cap?"

"The chief just gave it to me. It's part of my undercover disguise," he said.

"I think it suits you perfectly." She grinned and he laughed.

"Wait until you see my glasses with the big nose and fake mustache," he teased. She giggled and it struck her—she was joking with him about being undercover and she felt comfortable doing it. She'd dumped all undercover cops in one bucket and labeled it secretive, manipulative and underhanded. But Tucker kept surprising her and doing things that didn't fit the mold.

Before she could process her thoughts, Stella's voice caromed around the interior of the van. "Beckett and I have just pulled out. He's heading east on Green Avenue and I'm heading west."

"A black sedan just pulled in behind me, following close," Beckett responded. "I'll make some turns and see if he follows."

Tara glanced at Tucker. His fingers flexed open and closed on the steering wheel and his mouth was a firm line.

"This guy is shadowing me, move for move," Beckett said over the radio.

"I'm going to see if I can cut him off," Stella said. "There's no one suspicious behind me. Tucker, are you on the move?"

"Just getting ready to pull out," Tucker responded.

He brought the van to a stop at the street level, and the bright sunlight blinded Tara for a moment after the darkness of the parking garage. A couple cars whizzed by, and Tucker paused before leaving the garage. "Tara, lay down on the seat, just until I'm sure we're in the clear."

She nodded and slipped out of the shoulder harness on the seat belt to lie on the bench seat. She felt the vehicle jostle as the van pulled out onto the street, then the thrum of the engine sounded as they began to pick up speed.

"We're on the road," Tucker said into the radio. "So far, nothing suspicious."

"I'm behind you about four cars back," Katie reported. "I second Tucker. Nothing out of the ordinary."

"I just cut that sedan off at a light. Beckett, you should be in the clear," Stella responded.

"Status quo everyone, no changes until Tucker gets farther out of town and we're sure he hasn't picked up a tail," Marcus instructed.

Tara felt the van slow to a stop, and she peered up to see Tucker glancing left and right then pulling forward. Without warning Tucker slammed his foot on the brake, and Tara jolted toward the edge of the seat. In a split second he reached out and grabbed her, keeping her from tumbling to the floorboard.

"A blue Jeep, older model, just came out of nowhere, pulled in front of me and stomped on the brake, like he wanted me to rear-end him. He's moving forward now, and pulling away in a hurry."

"I'm going to circle around and see if I can get a look at the driver," Stella said.

"I wish I could see what's going on," Tara said. "I'm missing the action."

Tucker glanced down and smiled. "We're trying to avoid the action, pretty lady."

Tara's already elevated blood pressure rocketed to another level. *Pretty lady?* She tilted her head to see his face. From her position she could see the sharp angle of his jaw covered with a shadow of facial hair. The muscles moved in the column of his throat as he turned his head, his gaze traveling back and forth, taking in everything surrounding them. Tara said a quick prayer of thanks to God for bringing this brave, relentless man to her rescue.

"Tucker, I'm coming up on your right," Stella reported. "I see the Jeep."

"There's been no further erratic movement from him,"

Tucker replied, "but he's traveling below the speed limit now. I wonder if he's trying to bait me into passing him?"

Tucker nodded out the window, and Tara guessed Stella had just passed by.

A moment later, the female officer's voice filled the van. "He's wearing a baseball cap and talking on his cell phone, and it's blocking me from seeing his face. Looks like he has short, dark hair. He didn't look over."

"I'm going to pass him to see if he does anything," Tucker said.

A moment later, Tara could feel the shift in direction as the van moved around the Jeep and began to accelerate.

"I'm in front of him and have picked up speed. He's making no attempt to catch up," Tucker informed everyone.

"Sounds like a careless, irresponsible driver paying more attention to his phone call than the road." Marcus joined in. "Try and out distance him Tucker, but I think you might be in the clear."

"Tucker, can I sit up?" Tara could see blue sky out the window but nothing else.

"Not yet," he said as he reached out and gave her arm a gentle pat. "Just sit tight a little longer."

Tara felt her eyes close as the rhythm of the wheels on pavement created a soothing sound that enveloped her. Before she knew it, she'd fallen asleep, snuggled next to Tucker and momentarily free from danger.

Tucker glanced again in the rearview mirror, relieved to see nothing suspicious behind them. He stretched his neck left and right, allowing his body to relax. They were miles out of Houston on the way to Galveston Bay, and he was beginning to feel like they had dodged a bullet.

Tucker glanced down and he smiled as warmth spread

through him like warm molasses. Tara snuggled against him, her feet tucked under her on the seat. The soft sound of her steady breathing next to him was like a balm to his soul.

After Deacon's death he wouldn't allow feelings to surface and preferred to operate with a laser-sharp focus. But Tara was throwing him off his game. As much as her presence touched something he'd buried down deep, his lack of focus could be fatal. Soft little squeaks drifted from her lips as she stretched, and it took all his willpower to block out the sweet sounds and concentrate on their surroundings and the other drivers on the road.

Tara's entire body jerked and she sat up, scrubbing dark hair off her face. Shocked green eyes turned to him, and he could see the confusion as reality settled over her. She turned her head to look out the window, then glanced back at him.

"Where are we? What happened to the blue Jeep? How long have I been asleep?"

Tucker laughed. "Okay, let's see. On the highway to Galveston Bay. The Jeep turned out to be harmless. You've been asleep for about an hour."

She sucked in several deep breaths before twisting her torso and leaning back against the seat. "Not as comfortable as Stella's couch," she said, patting the fake leather she sat on. "But it works in a pinch. I tossed and turned in Stella's office all night. My mind was on a treadmill and wouldn't get off."

"The good news is we should be there in about an hour. We're taking a circuitous route just to make sure we aren't followed. I don't want to lead anyone to our doorstep," he informed her. "You can take a good nap when we get there. Scout and I will be on guard."

Tara's forehead wrinkled. "I appreciate you wanting to

be the superhero in all this, but you have to get some sleep too. Give me a gun, and I'll take a shift standing guard."

Laughter erupted before he could stop it and Tara turned in her seat, her arms folded across her chest and her head cocked to the side. "I told you I could shoot a gun. And if worse comes to worst, I can scream like a banshee. I guarantee you'll be up in an instant."

"That's an appealing offer." He bit his lips together to stop another burst of laughter. "I can't take you up on it. My job is to keep you safe, not sleep while you stand guard. I'll be fine. I went for several days at a time without sleeping when I was in Iraq."

Tara raised a dark eyebrow. "I didn't realize you were in Iraq. Army?"

He nodded, wishing he'd never mentioned it. "I flew choppers."

Her eyes widened. "That's an amazing skill. Why don't you still fly helicopters? What led you to being a K9 officer instead?"

Acid trickled into Tucker's stomach. He didn't discuss this with anyone except on rare occasions with Cade, who had his own scars from Afghanistan. He wasn't about to dump the guilt and remorse of what had led to Deacon's death right into Tara's lap.

"Let's just say I found something better suited to me. I get to work with an amazing dog like Scout, and we put bad guys behind bars. It's a winning situation." He glanced at her and she nibbled at her lower lip but didn't say anything further.

"Look, there's a little mom-and-pop restaurant at the next exit. Why don't we stop and get a couple burgers, and I can let Scout take a bathroom break and stretch his legs."

Tara nodded but kept her gaze on him. Her long lashes

fluttered several times before she turned and glanced out the window. He felt as if she could see through to his soul, and if he had to speak to anyone about Deacon, it shocked him to realize he would want it to be her. *What had gotten into him?* He shook his head to clear it. He had to get these wayward thoughts under control.

Ingrained habits from his military and police experience never died, and Tucker parked the van in a slot parallel to the restaurant so they could pull forward without having to back up. He put Scout on a leash and let him sniff in the grass for a few minutes to do his business while Tara poured water into a bowl for him. Once his partner was settled back in his kennel with a small portable fan trained on him for air, they headed toward the restaurant.

Without thinking Tucker grabbed Tara's hand and his steps faltered. Her fingers closed around his. "Let's go, Officer Dawson. I'm hungry," she laughed, and pulled him toward the door. What was it with this girl? She'd been shot at, almost blown up, and just about flattened by a semi-truck and she was still warm and personable. She tugged at him like no one else ever had, not even his ex, Rachel. It would take all his willpower to keep Tara at a distance, but he would not risk his heart. He'd survived that betrayal once. Never again.

She pulled him across the threshold into a brightly lit restaurant with stools at a linoleum topped counter and fresh baked pies in a refrigerated case. The sign at the entrance of the dining area said to wait to be seated, but Tucker had no intention of making them vulnerable by sitting in the middle of a restaurant, no matter how unthreatening it felt. Tara pulled her hand free and wandered over to a shelf that displayed homemade jams and jellies while Tucker placed their to-go order.

He glanced around the room as he pocketed his change, noting the fishing poles on the walls and pictures of men and women holding redfish, black drum and speckled trout from nearby lakes and streams. When he'd return to Galveston Bay from Iraq, he'd often leave his boat behind and take his kayak out, threading in among the marsh grass and throwing his line in. Dinner would be whatever he caught. The solitude had been healing. There would be none of that on this trip though. He didn't plan on leaving Tara alone for a minute.

Tucker turned to find her watching him, and she smiled and walked toward him. His heart thumped harder the closer she got. She placed a gentle hand on his forearm. "Do you like to fish? I saw you staring at those fishing poles with love in your eyes." She giggled and he sucked in a breath. The way she teased him made him feel like he'd known her forever.

"I do like to fish," he managed to get out. "I don't think we'll be able to do any of that on this trip."

Her lips lifted in a half smile. "Maybe some other time you can teach me."

Tucker swallowed a gulp, words trapped by a throat suddenly as dry as the Sahara. All he could do was nod before the waitress approached with their bag of burgers and fries.

Tucker's phone pinged and he placed the bag on a table and pulled it out of his pocket. "Marcus wants an update," he said as he texted a message to the chief. "We should be at the cabin in less than an hour," he told her as he pocketed the phone and retrieved the bag.

Tara gave him a thumbs-up and shoved the door open.

"Wait—" he began. He didn't want her leaving until he'd made sure everything outside was clear. He tossed a nod of thanks to the waitress as he hurried out the door. Tara had stopped short, and he pummeled into the back of her. He grabbed her shoulders to keep from knocking her forward. She remained rooted to the spot and he turned, following her gaze.

A blue Jeep pulled off the road, taking its time and coming to a stop at the far-right corner of the parking lot. Tucker jerked in a breath and his adrenaline spiked from zero to a hundred.

"Is it the same one?" she whispered. He could feel tremors rippling through her body.

"It's the same color, and an older model like the other one." He choked back the shock that rose like fire out of his gut. "I don't think this is a coincidence."

He noted with relief that at least the van was parked facing away from the Jeep. They were going to have to test that power the Houston PD said was under the hood.

"We have to get to the van. On three, you run. Get in on the driver's side. I'll cover you, and I'll be right on your heels." She nodded. Determination flared in her eyes.

Tucker whispered, "One…two—"

Tara gasped as a massive RV pulled into view and began a slow turn into the lot.

"Go!" Tucker said as the giant vehicle momentarily blocked them from the Jeep. Tara flew to the van, flinging the door open and diving across the seat. Tucker jumped in and started the ignition, throwing the vehicle in Drive and slamming the gas pedal to the floor. The engine hesitated for a moment, then shot forward with a squeal of tires. He expected the sound of bullets to ring off the van at any moment. Instead, the Jeep pulled out in no hurry, failing to keep up and disappearing into the distance as they left it behind.

Tucker glanced in the rearview mirror as he maneuvered

down a side street to get back to the highway. "Where did he go?"

"Do you think we were wrong about him?" Tara asked, eyes focused on her side mirror for any sign of the Jeep.

Tucker shook his head. Every warning bell in his arsenal was blaring. Something was not right. There was still no sign of the Jeep, and Tucker breathed in a lungful of air as the exit to the highway loomed ahead. "I don't think we're wrong, but I can't figure out what game he's playing. I hope this guy doesn't have a partner we're going to meet up with once we get on the highway."

He glanced over as Tara grabbed the takeout bag where it had landed at her feet and stuffed it behind her seat.

"Maybe we lost him," she murmured.

Tucker was about to reassure her when he noticed a dark vehicle behind them closing fast. He recognized the Jeep right away.

Tara glanced at him then jerked her head to the side mirror. "Tucker?" Her voice rose in alarm.

"Hang on!" Tucker swerved the van into the fast lane and hit the gas. The Jeep followed suit, gaining on them.

"How does he keep showing up?" she said with a shriek. Little threads of panic were woven through her voice.

He shook his head. "Million-dollar question. Tara, call 911. We're going to need assistance here."

Tara grabbed her phone to make the call. She put it on speaker and the emergency operator answered.

"We need help. We're being chased by some guy in a blue Jeep," Tara spluttered.

"Where are you located?" the woman asked.

"We're on Interstate 45 nearing exit 5," she said as Tucker

pushed harder on the accelerator. The Jeep continued to inch closer.

The operator's next question was drowned out by a loud explosion of bullets ricocheting off the back of the van.

SIX

"Get down!" Tucker shouted, as he veered back to the outside lane. Tara crouched low in the seat, whispering a prayer to God to keep them safe.

"What was that popping noise?" A voice sounded through the speaker. Tara had almost forgotten the emergency operator was still on the line.

"He's shooting at us, please hurry! We're in an electric company van. He's driving a blue Jeep." Tara glanced at her side-view mirror just as the Jeep swerved into the lane behind them.

"I'll get law enforcement to your location," the operator responded.

Another round of bullets hit the small window in the back of the van, shattering it, as Scout yelped.

Tara glanced back. Scout was on his feet in his kennel, shaking shiny pieces of safety glass off his coat. "Scout, sit," Tucker instructed, and the dog hunkered down.

Tara leaned back and closed her eyes, willing a calmness to settle over her despite the fear stampeding through her body. Drawing in a deep breath, she turned to Tucker. "Let me see your gun." His eyes held hers for a beat before he pulled it from the holster at his side. Her fingers closed around the Glock, testing the weight of the gun in her hand before rolling her window down. Tara's hair whipped into her eyes and she shoved it back, checking for other vehicles. She couldn't allow someone innocent to get caught in the cross fire.

"He's directly behind us," she shouted over her shoulder. "Ease to the left." Tucker moved the van over, and Tara leaned out the window and fired three shots at the Jeep, aiming for the right front tire. She jerked back inside. "I missed," she ground out in frustration.

Tucker reached for her arm. "Tara, it's too dangerous—" With a grunt she pulled away and leaned once more out the window, taking aim and firing again.

This time there was a squeal of tires and the Jeep twisted sideways. It spun several times before sliding off the road and coming to an abrupt stop, nose down in the ditch.

Tucker pumped a fist in the air and kept the gas pedal pressed to the floor. "That's my girl. Great shot!"

Tara leaned back into the seat as Tucker stabbed at a button on the radio to call the chief. The adrenaline rush was fading, but Tara's heart continued to pound out of her chest. *My girl.* It was just an expression. The last thing she wanted or needed was to be "the girl" of an undercover cop.

"Marcus, we've had some unwanted excitement," Tucker stated, briefing his superior on the events at the diner and ending with the perp spinning into a ditch. Marcus advised he'd contact the local authorities to get an ID on the suspect.

"I don't like that he knows what vehicle you're in," Marcus said. "We've seen more than one assailant throughout. He could have passed the information along to anyone."

"Agreed," Tucker responded. "I'm going to pull off at the next exit and do a search of our vehicle for anything suspicious. I could have sworn we'd left him in our rearview mirror when we departed Houston. We didn't take a direct route. How did he just show up in the parking lot where we stopped for food?"

The silence lengthened and Tara glanced at Tucker, wondering if the call had been dropped. Marcus spoke at last. "We all knew where you were heading. Maybe not the exact address, but the location of your cabin. There's not a soul on this team I don't trust, but…"

Tucker's fists tightened on the wheel and his mouth was a grim line. "I won't believe it's someone in our K9 unit."

"Until we can verify how this lunatic knew where to find you, I want you to communicate with me only."

"Understood," Tucker responded. His shoulders slumped, and Tara reached out and placed a hand on his arm.

"Update me after you search the van." Marcus disconnected the call.

Tara leaned closer, trying to get him to glance her way. "Tucker, I can't believe any of the officers I've met are capable of this. There must be something else."

"I'd trust every one of my fellow K9 officers with my life." His eyes were narrowed and hard. "You're right. There has to be something we've missed."

Tucker flicked on the turn signal and exited the highway, pulling into the corner of a large gas station and travel plaza. He yanked his baseball cap off and tossed it on the seat. Tara watched as he began a meticulous search of the van for anything suspicious. At one point he dropped out of sight as he got onto his back and shimmied under the van with a flashlight. He emerged with a streak of grease across his forehead that he tried to brush off with his arm. Tara leaned out the window with some paper napkins and he wiped at it, then tackled the dirt on his hands before wadding it up and throwing it into a nearby trash can.

"The van looks clean. I can't find anything suspicious."

He shoved his hands in his pockets and stared into the distance.

She rested her arms on the window frame. "Does it have to be one of your fellow officers? Is there anyone else who would have access to what's going on? A clerical person, or someone in IT?"

He shook his head. "Luca in IT is topnotch. The information he has access to is staggering, but his sister was killed by a gun smuggled into the country by a goon like Platt. He's on a mission to put these bad guys behind bars. And no one in clerical would have been in the loop about the discussion to hide out at my cabin." He scrubbed his hands down his face and turned to her. "We've overlooked something."

Tara nodded. "It's scary when you don't know who your friends are, who you can trust. That happened to Michael." She bit her lip as a tear trickled down her cheek. "He was a police informant, and his undercover contact seemed more focused on the outcome than in making sure Michael was safe and not compromised."

"I'm sorry you had to experience that," Tucker said. "Most of us who work undercover don't want the end result to be at the expense of the people involved."

Tucker's phone pinged, and he turned away as he pulled it from his pocket. Tara watched as he spoke to the chief, nodding his head, glancing at her, then nodding again. So far, he was as different from Evan Schenk as night and day. It probably wasn't fair to condemn all undercover officers because she knew of one who was more interested in getting ahead than in having the backs of the people he worked with. That profile didn't fit Tucker at all.

He ended the call, then climbed in behind the wheel and turned to her. "When the police arrived at the scene where the Jeep went off the road, the driver was gone. They combed the area, but he's disappeared. The vehicle was wiped clean with no identifying information. They're going to ask around at some of the fast-food places and gas stations in the area in the event anyone recognized a banged-up man without a vehicle loitering about their property."

Tara shuddered. "It's so sinister how he just appeared."

"I agree. But he's on foot without his vehicle, and we're soon going to be miles ahead of where he ran off the road. The plan is to continue to the cabin and travel with eyes in the backs of our heads." He smiled. "Marcus wants an update every hour on the hour and is notifying the Galveston PD to be on standby if we need anything. He's not giving them the location of the cabin at this time. The fewer who know about it, the better."

Tucker cranked the ignition. Before he could put the vehicle in Drive, Tara reached out and put a hand on his arm. He paused and turned in his seat to face her, his eyebrows raised and the hint of a smile on his lips. Her heart tripped over itself at the warmth in his eyes. "I'm sorry I lumped you into the same category as his police contact, Evan Schenk. You're not like him at all."

He gave her hand a gentle squeeze. "You're right. My top priority is keeping you safe. We're in this together. That's a promise."

She nodded. "I'm holding you to it."

"Then let's hit the road…again," he said, pulling out of the gas station and back onto the highway.

Tucker darted his gaze back and forth between the windshield and the rearview mirror so often he began to feel dizzy. Every car that pulled behind them sent a zip of alarm through his body. Staying hyperalert was far more exhausting than chasing a suspect on foot, and he craved a cup of coffee. Now was not the time. He wasn't about to take any more detours. It could wait until he got to the cabin.

He glanced over at Tara who was as vigilant as he was, her head on a swivel as cars rushed past them. A feeling like pride swelled within him at the memory of her leaning out the window and firing at their assailant's tires. What was he thinking? He clenched his jaw. She shouldn't be the one shooting at suspects. It was his job to protect her. But if she hadn't been so quick and accurate with his Glock, they might not be on the road now to Galveston Bay.

She was as brave as she was beautiful. Despite the danger they were in, there was a little thrill of excitement buzzing inside him that he hadn't experienced in a long time. He stole another glance at her before he could stop himself. Her hair was now hanging loose, and she'd plopped the baseball cap on her head. She took his breath away.

His cautious inner voice berated him. After Deacon's death and Rachel's abandonment when he'd needed her most, he wanted nothing to do with anything or anyone that made him feel too deeply. Now was not the time to dwell on what he was feeling. He should only be focused on keeping Tara safe.

He felt the touch of her eyes on him and that little thrill of excitement spiked. "Where'd you learn to shoot like that?" he asked, his voice sounding loud to his ears in the quiet of the van.

She turned to him, eyebrows at her hairline and her lips twisted to the side. "Not too shabby, huh?"

"Expert marksman I'd say," he responded, and she chuckled.

"One of my foster fathers had a thing about guns. He collected them. When other dads took their kids to the movies or to play baseball, Vic took Michael and me to the shooting range."

"At least he spent time with you." Tucker thought of his own father who'd left when he was six.

Tara nodded and glanced out the window.

"I didn't realize you were in foster care," Tucker said. Tara kept her gaze on the passing scenery. As the seconds ticked on, he began to think it was a sensitive subject, and she wasn't going to elaborate further.

"My parents died in a car crash when Michael and I were young," she said in a quiet voice. "We were in the back seat and managed to survive, but they didn't. I don't remember it, but Michael does…did…" Her voice trailed off. "Michael always wore Dad's dog tags after the car crash," she said, rubbing her thumb over the plastic case. "It helped him feel close to him after he was gone. Now I do the same thing to feel closer to Michael. At least I got to grow up with my brother. Until he and Vic had a major fight and Michael left at sixteen."

She shifted in her seat, angling toward him as her green eyes glittered with anger. "I was just getting to know him again when they killed him." Tara clamped her lips together and her chin trembled. "He'd gotten into some things he shouldn't have, but he was trying to make it right. He had dreams of one day going back to school to become a social worker. He had a real heart for kids who were struggling. He knew what it was like." Her voice cracked, and she turned her gaze to the endless trees whizzing past them outside the window.

Tucker reached across the seat and grabbed her hand, giving it a gentle squeeze. "He would be proud of how you're fighting for him, and for the people like Luca's sister whose families are suffering at the hands of someone like Platt."

Tara nodded. Her fingers tightened around his, and she let the silence lengthen. Tucker had more questions he wanted to bombard her with. Was Michael part of Platt's organization at one time? Was Tara? What kind of information did Michael have on Platt and did Tara know what it was? That would help to explain why she had a target on her back.

Once they got to his cabin and she was able to relax, he'd see if Tara would share more of what she knew with him. Then maybe this feeling of flying blind again in a dangerous situation would ease.

Without warning, images flashed through his mind, always when he was vulnerable and unprepared for them. The cocoon-like enclosure of the Black Hawk helicopter. The blades churning above him, and the vibration of the airborne machine that made him feel like every cell in his body was moving. The sight of smoke rising in the distance where he should be landing to pick up Deacon. The nausea that had coursed through him, intensified by the familiar cockpit smell of fuel and metal. If only he'd been there fifteen minutes earlier. But they'd delayed him…

Tucker shook his head and sucked in a breath, dragging himself with force back to the present. Tara's hand was warm in his, and he let the feeling of her presence steady him as his heart rate slowed to normal. He glanced at her out of his side vision. She continued to stare out the window, keeping her thoughts to herself. Tucker admitted he was feeling things for her that he shouldn't, but he couldn't go any deeper or any further. The feeling of heading into the unknown, unprepared, was like fleas crawling over his skin. He would keep her safe at all costs. But when the US Marshals Service decided on a plan, he would have to let her go without a backward glance.

SEVEN

Tara wasn't sure what she had been expecting at the first sight of Tucker's cabin, but what she was looking at was not it. From the outside it looked tiny. Maybe enough space for a living room and kitchen, but a bedroom was doubtful. It was lifted off the ground by four-foot stilts, and the space underneath looked ripe for housing spiders, snakes and numerous unsavory animals and insects. A sloping grassy expanse behind the house disappeared into the dark greens and browns of the swaying marsh grass. A soft breeze carried the scent of salty, slightly brackish water.

Tucker and Scout approached after having searched the property to make sure everything was secure. A grin split his face. "What do you think?"

"It's...great," she murmured, taking a longer look at the house and checking for holes in the bleached wood siding. "Um...there wouldn't be any critters lurking inside would there?"

Tucker laughed, a rich, deep sound that brought a smile to her face. "There might be, but I doubt it. I thought you were fearless. A little snake isn't going to scare you, is it?"

"Of course not! But a big one might." She sneaked another glance at the weathered cabin. "I think I'll let you go first."

"Right this way then, m'lady," he said, leading the way with Scout at his heels. Tara followed him up the wooden plank steps and waited while he unlocked the door. He and Scout stepped into the darkness. After a moment she heard the sound of a lamp being switched on and the clack of shutters pushed to the side of windows.

"All clear," he announced from inside, and Tara stepped across the threshold. She smiled without thinking and her shoulders sagged in relief. The living area was compact but except for a little dust, the furniture looked clean, as did the kitchen off to the side. A doorway did in fact lead to a small bedroom and bathroom. It was just the basics: sofa, chair, table, rugs on the floor. But something about it was cozy. And she needed cozy right now.

"It's perfect," she said, and meant it. Tucker's blue eyes glowed, and warmth spread through her body making her limbs feel loose. She suddenly felt too tired to stand and plopped on the sofa with a thud.

"I have a buddy who comes here once in a while to go fishing. He helps me keep the place livable and snake free," Tucker chuckled. "I know you're tired. Rest your eyes while I bring the groceries in from the car. Scout, stay with Tara," he instructed, giving her no time to argue as he headed outside. She leaned her head back and threaded her fingers through the thick fur at Scout's neck. Within seconds she was out.

Tucker bustled about in the tiny kitchen. It had always felt like a children's playhouse, with barely enough room to turn in a complete circle. He shoved the knob down on the toaster to heat up the buns, then pulled the burger patties and fries out of the small oven and set them on the stove. Not the best way to reheat hamburgers but it would have to do. He heard a soft movement behind him and turned to see Tara pushing hair out of her face and staring at him.

"Hungry?" he said, grabbing plates from the cabinet. She nodded and walked to the back door, unlocking it and stepping out onto the deck. He followed her, not only for her protection but also, frustratingly enough, because he liked being around her. She stared out at the marsh and he followed her gaze. The sun was beginning to set and the water that wove among the marsh grass was tinged with pink. This view always made the tension drain from his body and had brought him the peace he'd craved after returning from Iraq.

Tara pointed to a bluish gray bird taking off from the grass. "Beautiful!"

"That's a great blue heron. They're regulars here." He gave her arm a gentle touch. "Come on inside. Dinner is ready, and I'm not comfortable with you standing out here in the open, no matter how safe it feels right now."

"You're right," she said, following him inside. "But it's so peaceful. Looking at that view, I can't imagine anything more dangerous than a frog or a crab."

Tucker put a scoop of dry dog food into a bowl for Scout. Grabbing their plates and some forks, he led the way to the sofa. "Sorry, there's no kitchen table."

"This is fine," she said, sitting cross-legged on the sofa and balancing her plate. "Did this place bring you the comfort you needed after Iraq?"

Tucker paused, the burger halfway to his mouth. Had she read his mind a moment ago? He took a bite and chewed, not tasting his food as he thought back to his first days here. The struggle just to get out of bed. "It helped, after a time," he said, working to keep any emotion out of his voice.

He took another bite, trying to focus on anything other

than the weight of her eyes on him and how perceptive she was.

"I'm sorry for whatever it is you went through. Don't take this the wrong way," she said, her voice soft and low, "but I'm finding it so hard to believe. I can't imagine you as anything but how you are now, strong and capable. I'm on the verge of falling apart every ten minutes, and you're as steady as a rock."

Tucker felt as if the walls of the small space were closing in even further, and Tara was the only thing in the room. He wanted to tell her what happened in Iraq, unburden himself about Deacon's death, but the thought terrified him. He'd tried that with Rachel and had his heart sliced to ribbons. Before the awful details could hurtle from his lips, he lashed out at her. "I'm no hero. And I'm certainly not a superhero."

Tara's mouth dropped open, and he thrust himself off the sofa and retreated to the kitchen, taking deep breaths and trying to clear his mind of the nightmarish images. He sensed her behind him before he felt the warmth of her hand on his back.

"Whatever is burdening you is eating you up inside. God doesn't want you to carry that weight alone," she said.

He turned around to face her, placing his hands on her shoulders. "I should have known. Something was wrong, and I felt it in my gut but I didn't act on it. Don't you see?"

"What I see is that you need to forgive yourself," she said gently.

He let go of her shoulders and brushed past her. "Right. Because God forgives me I should forgive myself? I've heard that before."

Tara rushed after him and scooted in front of him, planting her hands on her hips. If he wasn't so flustered, he'd have laughed at her fighting stance.

"You may have heard it before, but you haven't listened to it." There was warmth in her eyes, honesty, but no pity. He felt the fight drain out of him.

Without thinking he lifted his palm to her cheek, captivated by the softness of her skin. His heart began to thunder out of his chest. He was losing ground and when she moved the tiniest bit closer to him, the floor tilted.

The sudden nudge of Scout's nose against his leg brought Tucker crashing back to earth, and he jumped back as the dog trotted to the door and stood at attention. Tucker shoved an unsteady hand through his hair and shook his head to clear it. "I'm sorry," he said, backing up. "Scout needs a bathroom break."

He opened the door and Scout scurried down the steps. Tucker turned and his eyes locked on hers. They were huge in her face, and she stood as still as a statue. "I'll be back in a second. I'm just right out here. Do not go anywhere," he said with a pretend stern expression that morphed into a smile when she rolled her eyes at him.

He stepped out into the twilight and breathed in a lungful of the salt-scented air. He had been about to kiss Tara, and that was wrong. He was here to protect her. His purpose had to be stronger than these feelings she was stirring in him. All these reminders of Deacon and his own failures were weighing him down, causing him to question his judgment.

He thought about what she'd said. That if God could forgive him, he should forgive himself. The trouble was, he'd never even asked God to forgive him. He'd been so mad at God that he'd shut Him out. Now it just felt too late. Best to just let that sleeping dog lie, he thought as he stepped onto the grass and watched Scout move farther out into the front yard.

* * *

The moment the door closed behind Tucker, Tara blew out a breath and dropped onto the sofa. Tucker had been about to kiss her, and what's more, she would have let him. She gave herself a mental smack. What was she thinking? Platt's men were out to kill her. She had to get out of this situation alive, and instead she'd been staring into Tucker's electric blue eyes, just waiting for his lips to touch hers.

Frustration coursed through her. She had to put the brakes on right now, but she was too agitated to sit still. Tara jumped up and walked into the kitchen, turning on the hot water and filling the sink with suds. Over the running water she heard the soft click of the back door. "Did Scout enjoy his potty break?" she said over her shoulder.

From the corner of her eye she glimpsed a dark, hulking figure. Before she could react, she was grabbed from behind and pulled against a wall of solid muscle. Tension and lethal energy vibrated through the man like an electric current. She opened her mouth to scream, and a hand clamped over her face, cutting off oxygen as she struggled, clawing at his hands to try and suck in air. Hot breath filled her ear, and a voice as cutting as a razor whispered, "Be still and do not make a sound, or I will kill you where you stand." There was not a fiber of Tara's being that doubted he meant it.

The barrel of a gun jabbed into her ribs, and he jerked her toward the back door and pushed her into the warm night. She stumbled on the steps leading down to the grass, and his arm clamped tighter around her neck as he continued to shove her forward. Every sense came alive, registering the denseness of the humid, salty air she was struggling to breathe, and the songs of the frogs and cicadas that were almost drowned out by his breath rasping in her ears. She strained to hear Tucker or Scout, but all was quiet. Had this man overpowered them before attacking her? The thought brought tears to her eyes, and she swallowed back a sob.

There was a way out; there had to be. Tara pushed back at the terror. "God, you go before me to fight for me against my enemies," she murmured.

"I told you, quiet!" His voice was laced with menace, and his arm tightened around her throat. Her eyes bulged as she struggled to take a breath.

If she could distance herself from the danger she was in, she could think more clearly. Tara concentrated on her surroundings to gather her bearings. He was propelling her down the hill toward the marsh. The moon provided some light, but she couldn't easily distinguish marsh grass from salt water in the dark. A horrified thought almost stopped her heart—he was going to drown her! She began scratching at his hand and guttural sounds erupted from her throat as she tried to scream. If he was going to kill her, she wasn't going to be quiet about it.

The butt of the gun slammed into the side of her head. Blackness crept around the edges of her vision, and bile rose in the back of her throat. The cold barrel of the gun pressed against her ear, and Tara closed her eyes. This was it. Tears spilled onto her cheeks. She had failed Michael.

Out of nowhere the night sounds of the marsh were broken by the bellowing of her name from inside the cabin and the deep bark that belonged to Scout. The tears came faster. Tucker was alive. Before Tara could react, the attacker hauled her over his shoulder and ran for the water. Her fists pummeled his back. She held her breath, waiting for the splash when she hit the water, and summoning the strength to fight him if he tried to shove her under. If she could escape, she could hide among the marsh grass.

All at once she felt the shocking sensation of being airborne, and she landed with a hard thud. Pain jolted through her body. What happened? Where was she? She tried to scramble to her feet and was jerked up and shoved down onto a wooden plank. Two oars were thrust at her. She dropped them and covered her ears as her attacker turned and fired shots toward the cabin. Tara stole a glance over her shoulder to get a look at the assailant. He was about as tall as Tucker with a heavier build and wore a long-sleeved camo shirt. A red and black ski mask covered his face. He turned around and pointed the gun at her back. "Row!" He turned and fired again in the direction of the bank. The boat pitched to and fro.

In the moonlight Tara could see Tucker racing down the hill, carrying a long object. The attacker fired again, and Tara's blood ran cold as Tucker dove to the grass. She held her breath until she saw Tucker scramble to his feet, grab the object and speed toward the water.

"Thank You, Jesus," Tara whispered.

Without warning searing pain slammed into her ribs as the attacker kicked her in the side. Tara shrieked and doubled over. The boat seesawed violently, and she leaned her head over the side, sure she was going to be sick. Hot breath burned her face as he crouched next to her. "Platt wants you alive," he said in a hoarse growl, "but if you don't get those oars in the water, I will shoot you now, dump your body over the side and deal with Platt myself." The evil in his voice turned her blood to ice. Tara knew Tucker wouldn't leave her. She had to stay alive to buy time to escape, so she would row. It was a struggle to sit upright, and Tara's fingers trembled as she slid the oars into the oar locks and began maneuvering the boat out into the water.

Tara heard a splash of water coming from the bank and her attacker fired again. She began praying in time with each stroke of the oars. Her arms burned, and with every breath she took, her side throbbed where he'd kicked her. But Jesus would give her strength and provide a way.

She saw movement on her right and a dark object slammed into the side of the rowboat. The little craft rolled back and forth and her assailant stumbled. His gun flew out of his hand and landed in the salt water with a splash. Without thinking Tara leaped up, momentum sending her flying over the side. She hit the water swimming, adrenaline and a determination to survive propelling her away from the boat.

The water felt heavy, and seaweed slithered around her legs. Salt water made her eyes burn, but she felt grateful to God for it. She'd gotten away. Tara slowed her strokes; she had no idea if she was heading back toward the bank or farther away from land. Treading water, she glanced around in the dim light to get her bearings.

A dark form moved slowly toward her, and she stifled a scream. Her attacker had seen her! She dove under the surface and changed direction. When she popped her head up again, she heard her name in an urgent whisper. Tucker!

"Right here," she said softly, as his kayak glided toward her. She was so relieved to see him she started to cry. He reached out and grabbed her arm, holding on to her with an iron grip.

"We have to hurry," he said in a hushed voice. "I'm going to keep the kayak steady. Can you climb onto the back and hold on to me?"

"I'm not sure," she whimpered. Her side throbbed, and darkness was creeping around her eyes.

"Tara, don't pass out on me," he said hoarsely. She watched as he grabbed a rope from the floor of the cockpit where he sat and looped it around her back and under her arms, then tied it with a sturdy knot to a bungee cord on the front of the kayak. "Hold on to the edge as best you can. I'll go slow, but I can't paddle without using both hands." His head swiveled in the darkness, on the lookout for the attacker in the rowboat. He began to paddle forward, keeping a constant eye on her and whispering her name over and over to keep her awake. Tara fought the blackness threatening to drag her under, but the soft movement of her body floating through the water was too much. Her head lolled to the side and she succumbed to the darkness.

EIGHT

Tucker untied the rope around Tara and lifted her into his arms. He hurried up the bank, slipping on the grass and then steadying himself. There was no sign of Tara's attacker, but Tucker wouldn't feel safe until they were miles away from here. How had they been discovered…again?

Scout emitted a soft bark at him from the bottom of the steps where Tucker had commanded him to wait. "Come on, Scout," he demanded as he climbed the steps two at a time. He rushed into the cabin, closed the door and locked it behind him. He laid Tara on the sofa and unholstered his Glock, clearing the small bedroom and bathroom to confirm the perp was not in the house.

He needed to contact the chief, but that would have to wait a moment while he made sure Tara didn't need immediate medical attention. There was blood and bruising from a cut on the side of her head, but that was all he could see. He gave her shoulder a gentle shake. "Tara, can you hear me? Nod if you can."

Her eyelids fluttered and a groan escaped her lips. "It hurts to breathe," she whispered. Her arm lifted in jerky movements as if controlled by puppet strings, and she rubbed her hand against her side before dropping her arm back down onto the sofa.

There was no blood on her shirt. She hadn't been shot. "Tara, I'm just going to lift your shirt up a tiny bit to see if there's an injury." He pulled the T-shirt a few inches above the waistband of her jeans and sucked in a harsh breath. The skin under her ribs was a mottled mass of red, purple and broken blood vessels. What had he hit her with? White-hot anger burned through him.

Tara grasped his arm, and tears squeezed out of her eyes as she struggled to sit up.

"Let me help," Tucker said, wrapping his arms around her and lifting her to an upright position. Tara suddenly jerked, grasping frantically for the chain around her neck. Her fingers latched on to it, and she shuddered out a deep sigh. "Thank goodness my dog tags weren't lost in the marsh," she murmured.

"That's good. I know those are special to you," Tucker said.

Tara nodded. "I think I'll feel better if I can get out of these wet clothes," she said shakily. "I don't suppose you have anything in a women's size six, do you?" She gave a small chuckle that came out as a sob. "I left the clothes Stella loaned me in the van."

She'd been through so much turmoil in the past half hour, but her sense of humor hadn't gone anywhere. His heart swelled. She was remarkable.

"Let me check. I'm not leaving you to go outside. Scout, protect," he said, pointing to Tara. The German shepherd trotted over and sat at Tara's feet. His long stride took him quickly to the dresser in the small bedroom. He found a few T-shirts and an old pair of gym shorts with a drawstring waist. These would have to do.

He rushed back to her. "I'm going to give the chief a call in the other room, but I'm right here if you need me."

She nodded as she took the dry clothes, and Tucker closed the door behind him. He pulled out his phone and hesitated. How did the assailant know they were here? They hadn't been followed. He was sure of it. The chief's concerns hit Tucker right in the gut, but this had gone beyond coincidence. Tara was too important to risk it, no matter what his feelings were concerning his team members.

Tucker dialed the number for the chief.

"Seever." His boss's brusque voice sounded in his ear.

Tucker wasted no time. "Marcus, he found us again."

There was a sharp intake of breath. "What? Are you both alright? Where are you now?"

"We're still at my cabin," Tucker said, launching into the details of the past hour. "He must have arrived in a rowboat through the marsh because that's how he was trying to escape with her. Fortunately, I had my kayak under the house so I could give chase. He lost his gun in the bay so I think he's without a weapon, but I wouldn't put anything past this guy."

"I'm sending the Galveston PD out there ASAP. You need backup in case he's still lurking around. And you're going to need another vehicle."

"Marcus, I know there are questions about who is involved in Platt's organization and our team has a question mark on its back. But Cade was with us when we were attacked on the highway, and he was a target too. He was run off the road, shot at and almost killed. I'd bet my life he's not involved with any of this."

The silence lengthened. "Alright, Tucker. I'll send Cade to your location. Hunker down tonight but be ready to leave first thing in the morning. I don't think the perp will show up with law enforcement crawling all over the property. Try and get some rest."

"Yes, sir," Tucker responded as the chief disconnected the call. He heard a sound behind him and turned. Tara's long, wet hair was tucked behind her ears.

"I jumped in the shower to wash the salt water off. I don't feel so sticky and uncomfortable anymore," she said with a half smile. "What's the plan?"

"We're going to wait here—"

"What?" Her voice rose an octave, and Tucker grabbed her hands.

"The chief is notifying the Galveston PD we need assistance, so reinforcements should be arriving soon. Meanwhile, Cade is on the way. We'll be leaving in the morning with him."

A frown pleated the delicate skin of her forehead. "Where will we be going?"

"Marcus didn't say, but somewhere we can keep you safe."

She pulled her hands from his and dropped onto the sofa. "No offense, but all the efforts so far haven't worked." She looked away and her shoulders drooped. "How do you evade someone who is always a step ahead of you?"

Tucker had no idea. He felt like he was letting her down. Grabbing a throw blanket that was draped over the sofa, he covered her with it, pushing the edges around her like a cocoon. "Here, you get cozy under this, and I'll fix you some hot tea."

She shoved the covering aside and bolted off the sofa, grabbing his arms and forcing him to meet her eyes. "Tucker, hot tea and a soft blanket aren't going to make this guy go away."

"I agree. But your nerves are shredded and so are mine." He heard the frustration, sharpening his voice and he took a deep breath. "I've got to think, try to figure out what we've missed. He's not superhuman. He's not invisible and can't walk through walls and listen in on our conversations."

Tara reached up and placed her hand on the side of his face. His blood zinged through his veins at her touch. "You're right, and I'm sorry. I know how hard you and the other officers are trying. I'd have been dead three separate times if it wasn't for you." The static in his nerves begin to dissipate. What was it about her that settled him, that made him want to lower his defenses?

"Just sugar," she murmured.

He blinked and pulled back, staring into her face. "What?"

"Just sugar in my tea, no milk." Her full lips tilted up at the corners.

"Got it." He nodded as he reluctantly stepped back and went to boil water on the stove. The faint wail of sirens sounded in the distance, and Tucker blew out his breath in a rush. It was about time.

Tara walked over and peered out the window. At least four police cruisers filled the yard. Their pulsing blue and red lights created silhouettes of the trees, cars and officers moving about and eerie, jerking shadows among the palm fronds. Tara shivered and rubbed her hands up and down her arms.

Tucker appeared next to her and placed a hand on her shoulder. Heat rushed through her body. "You sit down and rest. I'll make the tea after I speak with them." He nodded his head in the direction of the officers outside.

A sharp rap made Tara jump. "Sergeant Miller, Galveston PD," said a deep voice from outside. Tucker opened the door and the sergeant ambled across the threshold.

Tucker shook his hand. "I'm Officer Tucker Dawson and

this is Tara Piper. She was attacked and almost kidnapped earlier this evening."

"I spoke to Chief Seever, and he gave me a few details. Can I ask you some questions, Ms. Piper?"

Tara eyed the officer, wanting to believe in his honesty. After everything that had happened, she was afraid to trust anyone except Tucker. Even that was hard to do…to relax in the conviction that he didn't have a hidden agenda. She prayed she was right about that.

Sergeant Miller was not much taller than Tara, but he had the kind of bulk that indicated he spent much of his free time at a gym. His short blond hair was fading into gray, but his eyes were dark and shrewd. She hoped he truly was on their side because she suspected he was a formidable opponent.

"I know you've been through a frightening experience," he said, "but the more information we have, the better. An incident like this is unusual in our area."

Tara nodded and took a seat. "I'll do what I can to help."

Sergeant Miller sat on the edge of the chair, pulled out a notepad and jotted a few notes.

He began walking her through everything that had happened after she heard the back door click and was grabbed from behind. The images in her mind as she relived the events were harsh, and when she began to describe the moment she thought he was going to kill her, her breathing became so uneven Tucker made her stop while he got her a glass of water. Fury flared like hot blue coals in his eyes when she described how the masked assailant had kicked her in the side.

A knock sounded at the door, and Tucker excused himself to answer it. A young detective with a close-cropped haircut and wire rim glasses appeared in the doorway. Sergeant Miller motioned him in.

"This is Officer Perkins," the sergeant said, then turned to him. "Did you find anything?"

"There's no sign of anyone suspicious, and we did a thorough search. Some of the marsh grass at the bank appears to be trampled, so I suspect that's how he got onto the property. There's no sign of anything else unusual." The policeman shifted his weight. "There's a good chance we may turn up more information once the sun comes up."

"That coincides with my suspicions, that he arrived in the rowboat and dragged it onto the bank," Tucker told the two officers. "Some of the flattened grass may have come from me though, when I put my kayak in and got Tara out of the water."

Sergeant Miller moved to the door. "We'll maintain a solid presence outside tonight. In the morning we'll question some of the locals, see if anyone noticed this man. We'll also stop by some of the businesses that rent boats and fishing equipment and see if anyone remembers a stranger who rented a rowboat and didn't return it. I'd bet my lunch money that boat was either stolen or will be found with a hole in it at the bottom of the bay." He turned to Tara and his stern features softened. "In the meantime, try and get some rest. You've been through an ordeal."

Tara nodded. She felt a tiredness that leached into her bones, but she doubted she'd sleep. There were too many frightening images when she closed her eyes.

Tucker shut the door behind the officers, and Tara noticed that he turned the lock and then pulled on the door to test that it was closed tight. He gave her a smile and then walked to the kitchen. "Now for that overdue tea. You need something soothing after having to relive that."

Tara wrapped the blanket around herself and leaned back into the sofa. Her eyelids felt like weights were attached to them, and she fought to keep them open. In the end they won, and it wasn't until she heard the soft thud of a mug on the coffee table that they popped open again. She pushed herself up and reached for the steaming tea, bringing it to her lips and blowing on it before taking a sip.

Tucker settled into the chair across from her. "Once you drink that tea, you should try and rest. I saw those closed eyes when I brought it in here, and I was only out of the room a couple minutes."

"I am tired, but I don't want to sleep. I don't want to relive any of this. And I'm afraid to be unconscious and vulnerable. I have to remain alert, so I'm not taken by surprise. I'm a good fighter, and I like having that advantage."

He leaned forward, elbows resting on his knees. "I'm here, Tara, and there's a yard full of police officers outside. From now on you're not leaving my sight. Any bad guy is going to have to get through me, even Ski Mask Man." Tucker lifted his arm and flexed, then pointed to the biceps that bulged. "I call this 'the intimidator.'" He grinned.

She felt tension drain from her body. How was it possible that the only person she felt safe with was a handsome K9 officer who sometimes worked undercover?

"Why wouldn't you feel safe with an undercover cop?" Tucker asked, and Tara started.

"Did I say that out loud?" He nodded and heat crawled up her neck. She sipped at her tea, not wanting to meet his eyes or discuss it.

"I want to help you, Tara. It's my mission right now." He smiled, and her stomach wobbled at the dueling warmth and intensity of his gaze. "Any information you have about Michael, what he was involved in, even what it is about an undercover officer that gives you pause, it would help me to know."

Her fingers picked at the blanket, tugging at a loose thread. She hated the thought of being so vulnerable. But if it would bring Michael's killer to justice… "Okay," she said on a soft breath. "I'll tell you what I know."

NINE

Little fingers of guilt jabbed Tucker in the stomach. He knew he should be encouraging Tara to use this time to rest, but the guy they were dealing with was playing for keeps. Rage burned through him, molten and savage, at the way this vicious neanderthal had terrorized her. Tucker flexed his fingers slowly. He didn't want to alert her to any of the anger he was feeling. He needed her to share what she knew so they could figure out how this assailant was staying one step ahead of them.

Tara was taking some time to gather her thoughts. She looked small under the blanket, but he knew she wasn't weak or frail. There was a strength that radiated out of her and it drew him like a magnet. Her strength held hands with the fierce loyalty she had for her brother. Unlike Rachel, he knew she wouldn't have abandoned him when he'd needed her strength and support. He stopped short. Why was he even thinking of Tara in the same context as his ex-fiancée? He mentally stepped on the brakes.

Tucker guessed Tara would say her strength came from the Lord. He had heard her murmuring to God as he'd rowed them back to shore, before she drifted off. Something that almost felt like envy stirred inside him. He wanted that assurance that someone always had his back. God might be on Tara's side, but He wasn't on Tucker's.

A tear slipped out of the corner of her eye, and he resisted the urge to reach over and wipe it from her face. He wanted to give her some space to feel comfortable and open up about who and what they were dealing with, so he stayed still. She turned a watery gaze at him. "You can trust me, Tara," he said.

She chewed at her lower lip and nodded. "You're right. I know I can. Dan Cramer warned me against discussing this case with anyone. But it's not like you haven't risked your life for me over and over again." She sat up straighter and threw the blanket off, giving him a "get down to business" face that tugged at his heart.

"That's my girl," Tucker said, leaning forward. Pink crept into her cheeks and he was relieved to see some color back in her face.

Tara took a deep breath. "After Michael got into that fight with Vic and left at sixteen, I didn't see him for almost ten years. He would always send me a card on my birthday, but there was never a return address, and I had no idea how to reach him." She sighed and tucked her legs underneath her on the couch. "Then one day about a year ago, I was leaving work. I was a school guidance counselor in my former life," she said with a smile.

Tucker's eyebrows rose and he nodded. "I can see that. You'd make a great advocate and supporter for the students."

Pink dusted her cheeks once more and she shrugged. "Thanks for the vote of confidence." She picked up the blanket again, twisting the material between her fingers. "Anyway, there was Michael, leaning against my car with a huge grin on his face. We spent the entire weekend talking and catching up, although now that I think about it, he really didn't share details with me about what he'd been doing. Just that he'd gotten involved with a 'bad man.'" She made air quotes with her fingers. "But that he was getting the leverage to move on with his life."

"Did he tell you who this bad man was?" Tucker asked.

She shook her head. "Not at first. Then one day we were eating lunch at a burger place. I got up to go to the ladies' room and when I came back, there was a man at the table. I heard Michael tell him Platt had a ghost shipment leaving that night."

Tucker's blood chilled. A ghost shipment had to mean ghost guns—the guns traffickers built from kits and parts. Those guns lacked serial numbers and left law enforcement with no way to trace their origins. They were the perfect gun for committing a crime. Most often assembled in the US, they were then shipped abroad or to Mexico, or funneled into criminal markets in the US. Michael had gotten himself, and now Tara, mixed up in some deadly stuff.

"The stranger turned and when he saw me, he had a cross look on his face, but then it was gone. He smiled and said his name was Evan Schenk, and he was working with Michael on a project. Michael nodded in agreement, and everything seemed okay." She lifted her hands, palms up, and shrugged. "Evan pulled up a chair and joined us like he was part of the family.

"Not long after that Michael came by my apartment. He told me he may have to lay low for a while." Her voice thickened. "He didn't want me to think he'd disappeared from my life again. About a week after that I got a frantic call from Michael."

Tara sprang up so fast Tucker jumped. She paced around the small room, talking as she moved. "Michael said some bad things were happening. He said he'd been working undercover passing along information on Platt's organization to Evan Schenk, his contact in law enforcement. He was afraid his cover within Platt's organization had been blown."

Tara stopped and her eyes locked on Tucker. "He sounded scared to death. I told him he had to call Evan, that he needed police protection. Michael said he was a step ahead of me, but that it had gone to voice mail. He still hadn't heard from him. I begged Michael to go to the police station, or to come to my apartment. We'd figure it out." Her fingers shook as she shoved her hair off her face and dropped down onto the sofa. "He said coming to my apartment was out of the question. He couldn't risk leading them to me."

Tears trickled down Tara's face, and Tucker joined her on the sofa. He reached out and took her hands, holding them tight as her whole body trembled.

"I argued with him. 'Just come to my apartment, we'll fight them together.' He said I was the little sister, and he didn't have to listen to me." Her voice choked on a sob. "He always said that when I tried to order him around when we were kids. Then he asked me to hold on, Evan was calling. When he got back on the line, he said Evan had told him to wait there, that he was in the middle of something but would send one of the patrol officers to pick Michael up and bring him to the station. By the time the police officers arrived," she said, her voice shaking with anger, "they found him dead in his apartment. He'd been shot in the back of the head."

"Oh, Tara…" Tucker said.

"Evan called not long after Michael's funeral. He wanted to take me out to dinner, make sure I was okay." Her eyes bulged in disbelief. "He said it would be what Michael wanted. Someone to look after his little sister." Tara's eyes overflowed with tears. "I turned him down flat. If he'd done his job, there would have been no need for anyone else but Michael to look after his little sister."

Tara crumpled before his eyes, and Tucker grabbed her and hauled her against him. He pressed her head to his chest and held her close, rubbing his hand over her back. His heart was shredded at the pain she was going through, that she'd been carrying around for months.

No wonder Tara had an aversion to undercover officers. Acid curdled in his stomach at how Officer Schenk had been so callous about an urgent situation from a police informant.

Tara's sobs slowly quieted to an occasional jerky breath, but Tucker had no desire to release her. Her breathing soon became deep and steady and soft little snores puffed through her lips. He was reluctant to loosen his hold, but she needed some good sleep. He picked her up and carried her to the bed, covering her with a blanket. "Scout, protect," he said, and his partner found a comfortable spot on the floor. Tucker left the door ajar on his way out of the room.

The wind had picked up and he heard the sound of rain, a staccato of tiny hammers pounding the cabin's tin roof. Tucker grabbed Tara's mug and carried it to the window as he peered out into the yard. Even without the red and blue strobe lights he could see officers sitting in their cars. Two drenched officers assigned to guard duty plodded through the rain. The chief must have communicated something of the urgency in keeping Tara safe.

Tucker took a sip of the cold tea and his lips twisted. He moved to the kitchen and put the kettle on to brew another cup. There would be no sleep for him tonight.

Tara eased her eyes open, squinting at the washed-out light that leaked feebly through the closed blinds. Where was she? She turned her head and surveyed the room through narrowed eyelids. There was a small overhead light on the ceiling and pine walls. A small dresser painted dark blue stood in the corner. Nothing about it looked familiar, and her confusion grew.

She shifted on the bed and gasped. A dull pain throbbed in her side and memories flooded in at lightning speed. Panic coursed through her and she struggled to sit up, staring around the small room. Next to the bed, Scout sat with what looked like a smile on his face as he cocked his head to the side. Low voices sounded in the room outside the door. Tucker was talking to someone, but her clouded brain didn't recognize the voice.

Tara pushed the hair off her face and climbed out of bed, stretching to try and ease some of the soreness from her body. Even so, her legs wobbled as she moved to the tiny bathroom and splashed water on her face. There was a small toothbrush wrapped in clear plastic and a travel-sized tube of toothpaste and Tara reveled at being able to brush her teeth. She was beginning to feel human again.

On top of the dresser, she found a spare pair of jeans and T-shirt that Stella had given her. Tucker must have retrieved them from the van.

Tara stepped into the living room and Officer Perkins gave her a brief nod before heading outside. Tucker rushed over to her. "Good morning." His voice was deep and warm, and he held a mug of coffee. She sniffed appreciatively. "I guess that means you'd like a cup?" He smiled.

She nodded. "Yes, please."

"I'm glad you got some sleep," he said as he placed a mug filled with the hot coffee and a couple packets of sugar and powdered creamer on the coffee table. "Nothing too fancy here, but at least it's drinkable."

Tara dumped a sugar packet in the mug and inhaled the fragrant java before taking a sip. "This is wonderful."

There was a brief knock on the front door before it opened, and Cade's head appeared around the corner.

"Morning, Tara. It's good to see you up and moving about," he said as he ducked to clear the doorway. Rain dripped off his dark gray police issue raincoat. "If you can stomach that witch's brew Tucker calls coffee, you're stronger than most of the policemen out there in the yard."

Tara chuckled. "It's just what I need right now."

Tucker led Tara to the sofa and sat next to her while Cade leaned against the wall, arms crossed. Tara sat the mug on the table as reality descended around her. "What's up?" she said, noting the seriousness of their expressions.

"The police found the rowboat the assailant used," Tucker answered. "He untied it and stole it right off someone's dock. Other than that, there's no evidence to be found so far."

Tara's shoulders drooped. "So, no information that would confirm his identity or how he keeps finding us. Or even where he might be?"

"I'm afraid not." Cade shook his head.

"Then what do we do?" Her gaze flicked between the two officers.

"Marcus said the US Marshals' office believes they're getting close to locating the leak," Tucker said. "The plan is to get out of here and return to HK9 headquarters. Until we can figure out how the assailant is shadowing us, they want you at headquarters where security is tight."

"How are we supposed to get back there without encountering him again? He's playing cat and mouse with us. I don't like being the mouse."

Tucker and Cade glanced at each other, and the tension in Tara's body escalated.

"We're going to try and trick him," Tucker began. "Cade is going to leave in the van."

"I'm the decoy," the lanky officer smiled. "Between Shiloh and me, we'll hold him off."

"Meanwhile," Tucker continued, "you and I are leaving in Cade's SUV. One of the Galveston officers is going to follow us for a few miles to make sure we haven't picked up a tail. If everything goes as planned, we'll continue on to Houston. Without incident."

"I'm having déjà vu from when we left Houston yesterday. This maniac wasn't supposed to be able to track us then either. And how is he going to mistake Cade for you?" she said as her gaze bounced back and forth between the two. "You don't look like twins."

"Tucker's not that blessed," Cade said with a lopsided grin. He reached over to the coffee table and picked up Tucker's ball cap, placing it on his head. The tall officer's grin had disappeared, and his expression was sober. "We're going to try and fool him with this and hope he hasn't had a clear enough view of Tucker's face to notice the difference."

The plan seemed shaky to her. "What about me? Won't they notice I'm not in the van?" Tara winced at the skepticism she heard in her voice.

"It's not an ideal solution, but this situation has flip-flopped." Tucker shifted on the sofa so he could look her in the eye. "We thought isolating you would help keep him from locating you. But this perp is so unpredictable that isolation is now dangerous. We need you where you're able to be protected."

"The security at headquarters is tight. Only a few of us will know you're being brought back there," Cade added.

"Too bad I don't have a stunt double," she said.

"We're a step ahead of you," Cade said, and Tara blinked.

"One of Galveston PD's female officers is going to be your stand-in," Tucker responded.

Tara frowned. "I hate the idea of putting even more people in danger."

"I agree," Tucker echoed. "But it was her idea, and Sergeant Miller thought it was a good one."

"Okay, if you're sure." Tucker and Cade both nodded. "I guess I'm good with it then," Tara said, enjoying the crinkle of Tucker's eyes as he smiled at her. "I feel a little like a sitting duck, just waiting for him to strike. I'd rather be on the offensive."

"Then let's go," Cade said, pushing off from the wall and closing the door behind him.

Tara downed the last sip of her coffee as a sharp rap sounded, and Tucker peered out the door before admitting Sergeant Miller.

"I've been briefing officer Elaine Herrera. She'll be riding in the van with Officer Pritchard. From a distance I think the two of them could pass for you and Ms. Piper," he assured them. "The rain will only help make it easier to hide that you and Tara aren't in the van."

"Thank you for your help, Sergeant," Tara said. "I'm going to grab my phone charger from the van before they take off." Tara rushed out the door, smiling at the pretty, dark-haired officer who was talking with Cade.

The rain was cool and invigorating and Tara wiped the dampness from her face, dodging puddles as she went. She leaned into the van and reached across the seat for the phone charger. A shimmer of something lodged under the windshield wiper caught her eye, and her heart thumped to a stop before taking off at a gallop. It hadn't been there yesterday. Tara grabbed the little plastic sandwich bag from underneath the wiper. There was a folded piece of paper inside.

Gingerly, she pulled the seal apart and reached in, unfolding the note. Her knees nearly buckled and she dropped onto the seat, staring at the mismatched letters and childish script:

ALL IS QUIET IN THE MARSH
IN THE DARK I RESIDE
THE MOON LOOKS DOWN,
THE STARS COME OUT
AND YOU DEAR TARA CAN'T HIDE

Always Watching,
Your Brother's Killer

Tara couldn't move. It was as if she was covered by a lead blanket. Before she could blink, Tucker was there. He grabbed the paper from her hand, and she watched as his eyes became saucers and his nostrils flared. He was saying something to her because his lips were moving, but the words were formless and came from a long way off. This man who was hunting her was from some horrific nightmare, and he was not going to stop. She wanted to collapse under the weight of the fear. He was the one who'd killed Michael. That meant she had to stop him first.

Tucker grabbed her and pulled her from the vehicle. His arms encircled her, strong and comforting. Sudden tears sprang to her eyes and mixed with the rain pelting her in the face. She wasn't in this alone. God was her strength. And He'd sent Tucker to help her. How else could she explain his presence and the sacrifices he was making for her?

Tucker pulled back and looked into her eyes, brushing her damp hair off her face as he pulled her to the porch out of the rain. "Are you alright? This maniac is toying with you. He's trying to get in your head."

Tara nodded. "It almost worked. But I'm okay. I'm grateful God brought you into my life to help me. I'm sorry if I've put you in danger too."

"Don't worry about me. We're going to get this guy Tara. One way or another we're going to take him down." Tucker's eyes were blue steel and when he pulled her close, she sank into him, allowing herself the solace of feeling safe in his arms. He wasn't just a delight to her eyes. He was compassionate and brave, and a fierce protector. Her heart was becoming attached to him, and she was surprised to realize that didn't scare her. For the first time she allowed herself to believe he was 100 percent in this with her.

TEN

The rain was coming down in sheets, but Tucker kept his foot at a steady pressure on the gas pedal. A sense of urgency had taken root, humming under his skin. It would have been better if they'd had a Houston PD helicopter to bring them back, but the heavy rain and wind that morning had caused the chief to decide against it. At least conditions were somewhat better now. He would not take an easy breath until Tara was safely back at headquarters. Despite the sleep she'd gotten the night before, the skin under her eyes looked shadowed and puffy. The combination of fear and grief were taking a toll.

Cade and Officer Herrera had pulled out about an hour before them, in the hopes the perp would follow the van and be well away when Tucker left with Tara. The plan made Tucker uneasy. The attacker had been able to evade the officers to put a note under the windshield wiper. Had he seen Cade and Herrera get in the van?

Tucker was taking a different route from Cade, per orders from the chief. Seever reasoned this back road was not as predictable a route as the highway Cade was on, so the assailant and any possible cohorts wouldn't be watching for them on this long, two-lane stretch of asphalt. But

Tucker knew there was less opportunity to blend in or get help out here.

The chief had checked in a short while ago, reporting that so far Cade and Officer Herrera had encountered nothing unusual. Tucker was relieved, but also a little concerned at the news. Did this mean the perp hadn't fallen for the decoy plot and wasn't tailing them at all?

Tucker glanced once more in the rearview mirror. The road barreled in a straight shot alongside marshes and bayous but wasn't so isolated that they didn't see the occasional truck or car, headlights appearing out of the gloom before whizzing past. His blood pressure ratcheted up with every vehicle they encountered. He kept his speed right at the limit, thankful when vehicles coming up behind their SUV decided to pass rather than follow behind, even as he marveled at their recklessness on a rain slick back road. Tucker shifted in his seat and rolled his shoulders, trying to ease the strain. He was on edge, and wished for the hundredth time they were already back at headquarters.

"We just lost Officer Kerns," Tara said as she looked in the side-view mirror.

Tucker glanced behind them to see the Galveston officer who'd tailed them for the last twenty miles turning around and heading back the way he'd come.

"I guess he feels like there's nothing out here but us and the occasional car zipping past."

"Have you even looked at the countryside?" Tara pointed out the window. "I half expect to see an alligator come crawling up the bank and onto the road."

Tucker chuckled. "They're more afraid of you than you are of them."

Tara's eyes popped. "Not last I heard," she said, and turned to stare out the window. Apart from the rain pounding on the roof of the SUV and Scout's snoring, all was quiet, and Tucker breathed deeply, trying to relax.

He stole a glance at Tara. Her gaze was focused on the wet landscape outside the window, looking for alligators no doubt. He smiled. Everything about her captivated him, from her sense of humor, to her bravery, to her loyalty to Michael. That it was all wrapped up in a beautiful package was just the cherry on top.

She turned her head and caught him staring. Color crawled up his neck and fanned out into his cheeks. Tucker hoped in the gloom she couldn't see his face turning the color of a beet.

She lifted her lips and turned in her seat to angle her body toward him. "I've been thinking."

"Is this where my eyes bulge and I cover my mouth in alarm?"

She laughed, a soft, husky sound that sent his pulse racing. "No, it is not. You've saved my life at least three times, and you know more about me than I've shared with anyone. Ever." She hesitated and Tucker waited, not sure he wanted to hear the rest of the thought.

"Would you tell me a little about you?" she said. "You know, to pass the time."

Tucker's heart pounded against his ribs. The last thing he wanted to do as he was driving her to safety down this rain-slick road was to tell her about his life and his failures. She trusted him. What would she think when she heard about Deacon?

He shoved his fingers through his hair and stalled for time. She nodded and smiled. It appeared being trapped in a car with her meant she wasn't going to let him get out of this.

"There's not a lot to tell," he began. "I was an only child. I had an uneventful childhood until my dad decided he didn't want to be with my mom anymore, and I got dumped into the discard pile too." Amazing how much that still stung, he thought, swallowing against the sudden lump in his throat. Tara's eyes were filled with warmth. She reached over and laid a hand on his arm and gave it a gentle squeeze. The tiny gesture was like water to that parched piece of his soul. How did she seem to know exactly what he needed?

Tucker took a deep breath. "Everything continued as normally as it could after that. Mom got a job, I stayed in school. I wanted to go into the military from as far back as I can remember. In high school I went with a bunch of my buddies to the beach over spring break, and they dared me to take a helicopter ride. When it shot out over the ocean, I thought I'd lose my lunch." He chuckled, remembering the roar of the powerful rotors and the feeling of being in a rattling tin can with windows. "Then the pilot skimmed across the water, and you wouldn't believe the colors you can see from above. It was surreal, like being part of the earth and the sky at the same time. I knew right then I wanted to fly choppers."

"I'd have been curled up in my seat, covering my eyes and praying to step on solid ground again," she laughed.

He reached over and grabbed her hand. "I'll take you up one day. You'll change your mind."

"Maybe," she giggled, and linked her fingers through his. Heat burned through him like warm honey. If she'd been waiting for him when he got back from Iraq, how different would his life be now?

Tara twisted toward him and tapped his cheek with a gentle finger. His brain skidded back to the present. He took a quick glance in the rearview mirror, relieved to see nothing behind them, then shifted his attention back to her.

"If you love flying helicopters, why did you quit?"

Tucker shrugged. "I already told you. I wanted a change, and I get to work in a K9 unit now."

"I know," she said. "But why did you really quit?"

He stole a look in her direction and the affection in her eyes undid him. Before his brain gave permission, the harsh truth he'd tried to avoid tumbled out in a rush of words that carried him back in time five years. How he was working search and rescue and had known something was wrong from the message he'd received from Deacon, urging Tucker to make haste as he'd gotten separated. How Tucker had been ordered to go to a different location to pick up a soldier, but signals had gotten crossed, and the wounded soldier had already been rescued when he got there. How he'd defied orders to return to base to refuel first and instead had flown to where Deacon was hunkered down, only to find out he'd arrived too late.

In private they'd read him the riot act for not following orders. In public they'd given him a medal for recovering the body of a fellow soldier who was in enemy territory. It was only later he learned the wounded soldier was the nephew of a state senator. Tucker knew in his head that soldier deserved to be rescued too, but the delay had caused the death of his friend. He'd returned home emotionally bruised and battered. His fiancée had said he'd changed and given him back the ring.

He felt Tara settle her hand on the back of his neck. He knew she meant it to be comforting, but guilt racked him and he avoided her eyes.

"Not only did people abandon you, do you think God did too because your prayers weren't answered and Deacon died?" Tara's voice was soothing, and he let it cauterize his raw nerve ends.

"I did, and I still do," he said after a moment.

"Tucker, God doesn't play favorites, even if it sometimes seems like it. Everyone is in a different place in their walk with Him. And everyone goes through valleys." She moved her hand, and her fingers gripped his shoulder. "He wants you to let Him take your hand as you go through the hardships, not push Him away."

"I've heard all this before, Tara." He stared out the windshield as a red pickup truck headed toward them in the oncoming lane, whizzing past and spraying their vehicle with water. The SUV swayed on the slick road. Tucker gripped the wheel tighter, glancing in the rearview mirror to see the truck disappearing behind them. Guilt was tearing at his insides, over Deacon and over his sloppy decisions in this case. He wasn't doing his job right now. He'd been reliving the past, and they'd almost gotten blown off the road by a reckless driver.

"Well, then, maybe you need to hear it again," she said. He turned a startled glance at her. Her lips lifted into a smile, taking the sting away from the words. "I'm not having an easy time of it, am I? I've lost my parents, my brother and on several occasions, I've almost lost my life. I've been angry and shouted at God." She lowered her gaze. "And then asked for forgiveness," she said, her voice a whisper. "But I've never felt God abandoned me. He's giving me a way through, and you're part of it."

He glanced at Tara. Her eyes were wide and earnest, and he sighed. "I'll give it some thought." Tara's eyebrows hitched up. "I will, I promise. Once you're safe and I can focus on it."

Tucker turned his gaze back out the windshield. The rain shimmered on the asphalt. The trees and marsh grass looked soggy and weighed down, just like he felt. His gaze darted to the rearview mirror again and his heart stopped. Behind them the red truck spun in a U-turn and began racing toward their vehicle.

Tucker slammed his foot to the floor and the SUV shot forward. "Tara, hold on!"

Tara didn't have time to react. The SUV shuddered at the explosive crash of metal from behind. The bone-jarring collision launched her toward the dashboard before the seat belt slammed her back into place. Their vehicle fishtailed as Tucker tried to control the tires on the wet pavement. He floored it again, and they shot forward with a squeal of tires.

Tucker jabbed at the radio and it crackled to life. Not waiting for dispatch to respond, Tucker shouted, "This is Officer Dawson. Notify Chief Seever the perp is back. We've just been rear-ended and are trying to outrun him."

Tara twisted in her seat to look out the back window at the oversize truck. She could see its silver grille dwindling in the distance. The red monster seemed to be disappearing behind them in the downpour. "Tucker, I think he's backing off," she said on a shaky breath. Scout yipped and Tara was relieved to see the dog hunkered down in his kennel.

"No, he's not," Tucker growled. Tara scanned his grim face, and unease churned in her stomach. "He's drawing back to accelerate and ram us again."

Her heartbeat slammed in her chest as the seconds ticked by. Tara kept her eyes on the spot where the truck had vanished in the gloom. There was nothing but rain and haze. Then she heard the faint rumble of an engine revving and stared in horror as the truck appeared out of the mist and barreled forward. She could hear its engine screaming as it sped toward them like a ferocious animal, closing the gap between them with deadly efficiency.

"I have nowhere to go," Tucker shouted. "Hang on!" Tara

sucked in a breath and squeezed her eyes shut moments before the thunderous crash from behind. The nauseating sound of metal crunching against metal filled the interior. The SUV careened out of control, and Tara screamed as they spun like a top across the slick asphalt. The earth tilted at a sickening angle, and they crashed through bushes and tall grass. The SUV plunged nose first into the marsh, stopping with a turbulent thud before the vehicle settled onto the boggy ground. Brackish water began to seep in around the door. Tara jerked in a strangled cry and grabbed at her seat belt buckle in a panic.

"Tara." Tucker held her face between his hands. His blue eyes were intense. "We're not going to drown. We aren't that deep in the water. It's not up to the rear door. But he'll be coming. We have to run. Now."

Tara nodded and sucked in several quick breaths. "Dear God, please help us, please help us," she murmured.

Tucker climbed through to the back of the vehicle, bringing Tara with him. He jabbed the K9 door remote, pulling Scout through the opening and into the murky water. "Scout, go." Tucker pointed to the bank and the dog took off paddling.

The warm water was at waist level. Slimy plants wrapped around her like a mummy's bandages. She tried to push forward through the murkiness, but her legs felt like lead, weighed down in the muck that suctioned around her feet and threw her off balance. Tucker grabbed her hand, dragging her along. Her legs were on fire from the exertion through the heavy, suffocating water. Tara glanced around nervously for the presence of a snake or an alligator, the hum of mosquitos loud in her ears.

Tucker jerked to a stop and turned his head, listening. The swoosh of tires on wet asphalt came to an abrupt halt. The rumble of a powerful engine idled, then ceased. A heavy door slammed, followed by the sound of unrelenting foot-steps on gravel, and Tucker tightened his hold on Tara, half pulling and half lifting her onto the far bank. She slid in the wet grass and fell forward, landing hard on her knees. Tucker jerked her up, and they crashed through bushes and tall grass, the trees a blur as they whizzed past. Brambles tore at her jeans. Tucker tripped over a thick root and Tara crashed to the ground with him. The sound of a gunshot rang out, and a bullet slammed into a sapling next to them.

Tara scrambled to her feet, grabbing Tucker's arm and running for cover behind a larger tree. She skidded behind it and Tucker stepped in front of her, covering her body with his. He pulled his gun from its holster and peered around the tree. More gunshots sounded, and bark exploded next to Tucker's face. Tara stifled a scream.

"I can't see him," Tucker huffed, his chest rising and falling rapidly. "Between the rain and the gloom, he could be anywhere."

Tara tried to catch her breath. "I can't hear anything ei-ther."

Next to them, a low growl rumbled in Scout's throat and the dog stood, eyes focused on a large clump of bushes to their left. Tucker took aim and fired. A sharp cry and a string of curses rang out.

"Move!" Tucker ordered. Tara sprinted forward through the wet undergrowth. She almost tripped in a deep puddle but managed to stay on her feet. "Go, go!" Tucker yelled as he paused, firing again in the direction of the bushes.

How could he have found us again? Tara pushed back the panic and concentrated on the terrain and staying on her feet. Rain splattered her in the face, and the pain in her side where the attacker had kicked her felt raw and irritated, as if covered in hot sand. Breathing was becoming an effort. *Just one more step, just one more step.*

She heard Tucker behind her, matching his pace to hers and shielding her from the gunman. He sprinted next to her, taking her arm and pulling her with him against a large cypress tree. Tara's chest heaved and his eyes roved over her.

"Are you alright?" he said between breaths.

She gave him a thumbs-up.

"We have to keep going. Looks like there's a path up ahead, which means it could lead somewhere we might find help, or even better, back to the highway."

"Let's do it." She nodded.

"That's my girl. Scout and I will be right behind you."

Tara pushed away from the tree. Her legs felt like rubber, barely able to hold her up, and she almost pitched forward before getting her feet under her. Without warning she heard a crash behind her and a loud grunt. She skidded to a stop and pivoted to see Tucker sprawled facedown on the ground.

"Keep going." His voice was a hoarse whisper. "I'll catch up," he said, struggling to get to his feet. Tara grabbed him around the waist and helped him up. He took a step and sucked in a sharp breath, his lips twisted in pain.

"I think I twisted my ankle," he panted.

"Let me help you." She tucked herself under his arm, keeping a tight grip around his waist. "Hold on to me," she said.

"Absolutely not," he said with a scowl. "Me hobbling along is just going to slow you down."

"I'm not leaving you," she declared. "We can stand here and discuss it, or we can start moving."

Tucker huffed out a breath and nodded. "Fine, just until I work it off."

They kept a constant pace, and Tara focused on the steady

rhythm of Tucker's breathing. A bullfrog croaked in the slow-moving water about twenty yards away and birds chattered overhead, but there was no sound from their attacker.

"Where do you think he is?" she said between breaths.

"Million-dollar question. Hopefully he's injured and is nowhere close by, but I'm not betting on it. Here's the trail," he said as they stepped onto an overgrown path. "I think I'm okay," he added, pulling away as Tara let him go. He still had a slight limp, and she could see the clench of his jaw.

"After you," he said, and Tara increased her pace. She could only pray they had left the gunman behind.

ELEVEN

Tucker's ankle throbbed and he gritted his teeth in frustration. How much time had they lost because he'd had to have Tara help him? He thought back to the fierce determination in her eyes when she'd refused to run ahead. Her strength and loyalty touched places in his heart that he'd kept under lock and key for a long time.

Tucker shoved a vine out of his path and cringed as it dumped more water on his head. It concerned him they hadn't heard any sounds from the gunman. Over the rain and the wind, he wasn't sure he would even hear the assailant before it was too late. He could only hope the shooter was disabled and unable to follow them. Tucker glanced at Scout. His partner trotted next to Tara and showed no signs of alerting to anything sinister.

He suspected there would be paths through this bayou leading to piers or fishing shacks where they could take cover. It would be even better if they stumbled on one that led to the highway. Knowing the chief, an army of reinforcements would be on the way if they could just make it out of here.

The gloominess under the canopy of trees began to give way to lighter surroundings, and vegetation thinned out. They were coming into a clearing and Tara glanced over her shoulder, slowing her steps. A narrow wooden bridge, barely wide enough for two people walking side by side, stretched high above the water. Tara came to a stop.

She glanced at him and then back at the bridge. "It doesn't look safe." Her voice quavered.

"Tara, we've been run off the road and shot at by some crazed attacker in a pickup truck. It has to be Ski Mask Man. This bridge is tame in comparison. Let's go. We can't stop now." He grabbed her hand to pull her along and found himself jerked off balance as Tara dug her feet in, unwilling to move.

"Look at it," she said as she pointed to the weather-beaten wooden planks. "Most of the side rails are gone. The boards may not hold us, and that's a long drop to the water."

It dawned on him in a flash. Tucker tipped her chin up. Rain ran in rivulets from the top of her head onto her face. Her clothes were a second skin. He pushed her wet hair back so he could look into her eyes. "Are you afraid of heights?"

Tara bit her lip and held her thumb and forefinger an inch apart. "Just a little bit. You don't know how deep that water is below the bridge. If it's too shallow, we could be seriously injured."

Tucker didn't want to admit it, but the bridge gave him pause as well. There were gaps across the length of the bridge where planks were missing or broken, and the wood could be rotten. It was only maybe a fifteen-foot drop, but Tara was right—if the water was shallow, they could break a leg. But there wasn't another option. They had to keep moving forward since the gunman could be right behind them.

"There's a secret to it," he said, moving in close, his face inches from hers. "We hold hands as we cross."

Her green eyes were wary, but before he knew what was happening, she closed the distance and pressed her lips to his. They were wet and warm, and his heart exploded in his chest. Their breath mingled in the rain for the briefest of moments, and then the kiss was over. She stepped back, her cheeks full of color. "I'm ready now," she said. Drops of rain dripped off the end of her nose and he brushed at them, then took her hand and led her to the first plank.

He gave her fingers a squeeze. "Don't look down. Just hold on to my hand and keep moving forward."

She nodded and they started out onto the bridge. The decaying wood creaked beneath their feet, and Tara shot an intense stare his way. Tucker could feel the tension in her body and his body echoed it, but they had to move with a purpose.

Scout stopped abruptly, a deep growl rumbling out of his throat, and Tara sucked in a sharp breath. Tucker dove onto the rickety wooden boards, taking Tara with him just as the crack of gunfire sounded and bullets whizzed over their heads. "Stay down," he yelled, adrenaline rocketing through him. He twisted around into a crouch position and fired several bullets in the direction of the gunfire, scanning the dark green depths for movement. A gleam of metal flashed through the trees and stopped near a cypress. Tucker fired again.

"Tara," he hissed over his shoulder. "Get ready to run! Scout, protect!" The dog stood at attention, his gaze riveted on Tara.

She grabbed Tucker's sleeve. "I'm not leaving you here."

"I'll be right behind you. Take off on three. One…two… three!" Tara scrambled to her feet, Scout at her heels as Tucker fired into the trees. He jumped up, his feet pounding as he sped across the weathered planks of wood. Tara was almost to the other side when Tucker heard a sickening crack and felt himself plunging through the splintered gap of a rotten board. Instinct took over and he grabbed at the wet boards with both hands, growling in frustration as he heard his gun splash into the water below.

His legs flailed in midair, and his fingers burned as he struggled to keep his grip on the slick, wet board. The thump of her feet running back from the far end of the bridge vibrated over the old planks, and Tucker fought to hang on. He looked up to see Tara, her eyes filled with panic and her face white as a sheet.

She crouched and reached for him. "Give me your hand!"

"No…keep going! He'll be coming." Gravity was working against him. The weight of his body pulled him down toward the water and made speaking difficult.

"Tucker, give me your hand. I'll help pull you up," Tara hissed.

"I'll pull…myself up. You can't lift me," he panted.

"Watch me," she said. Determination flared in her eyes, and she reached for his arm. A bullet whizzed over her head, and Tara flattened herself to the wood.

Sudden, white-hot pain ripped through Tucker's side, and he grunted, using every ounce of willpower to keep his handhold on the wooden plank.

Tara shrieked. "Tucker, you've been shot!"

"Tara, there's no time…you have to leave me behind. Go! Get across the bridge."

Her eyes bulged and she shook her head. "No, we stick together."

"My fingers are slipping. I can't hold on. You jump first then. I have to make sure you're safe."

The sound of gunfire echoed through the sodden air, and a hail of bullets whizzed by. Tucker tensed, expecting another bullet to rip into his flesh.

"Tara, you and Scout jump now! On three." His side was on fire, and there were two blurry images of Tara when he looked at her. "One…two…three!" He heard a small splash followed by a larger one. His fingers released their grip, and he let his body drop into the water.

Tara surfaced, coughing and wiping the dense, murky water out of her eyes. Scout popped up next to her, and she pointed to the far bank. "Scout, go," Tara instructed, thankful Tucker's partner listened and followed her command.

She twisted in the water, desperate to locate Tucker. His head appeared above the surface and his eyes darted frantically, finding her and swimming toward her. She threw her arms around him and held on for dear life. "Are you okay?" she said in his ear, choking back a sob.

"Don't worry about me," he said, holding her tight against him before pulling back. "We're going to swim to the bank where Scout is. Stay under the bridge. It's some protection and we'll be a harder target to hit."

"Got it," she whispered, and began pushing through the muddy water. *Give us strength, God*, she prayed, keeping her eyes on the bank as if it was the pot of gold at the end of a rainbow.

All was quiet except for the sound of their breathing and the soft splash of water as they swam. Tara heard a noise and her breath caught. She darted a glance at Tucker. He'd heard it too because he stopped swimming to listen. The muffled sound of footsteps approached at a run, then the assailant bounded on to the bridge, pounding closer to them over the rickety boards. Tucker reached out and grabbed her arm. "When he gets close, dive under."

"Okay," she whispered. Her heart thumped harder with each footfall that sounded on the bridge.

Now, Tucker mouthed, and she held her breath as he pulled her beneath the surface. Seconds ticked by. She couldn't make out anything. It was like looking into a brownish-green cloud. Just when she thought her lungs would burst, Tucker tapped her shoulder, and she peeked out of the water.

Tara heard the footsteps reach the end of the bridge and stop. Tucker placed a forefinger over his lips, and she nodded. Without warning the stillness was broken by a sudden deep growl. Tara turned to the bank in time to see Scout race toward the bridge. There was a loud thud as the perp landed hard on the ground, then the deafening sound of a gun blast.

"Scout!" Tucker cried, and pushed through the water with urgent strokes. Tara followed, plowing through the water behind him. "God, protect Scout," she whispered, fighting back tears.

The guttural sounds of grunts and cursing could be heard over the dog snarling, then Scout yelped. The sound of feet pounded the ground at a hard run. By the time Tara clawed her way through the sticky mud onto the bank, the perp had disappeared through the bushes.

Tucker was hunched over his partner and nausea skittered through Tara. She ran, skidding to the ground next to him.

Tucker's eyes were closed, and his chest heaved as he sucked in gulps of air. Tara glanced at Scout, and he gave her a weak tail wag. "Scout's alright?" Tara asked, rubbing her hand over the dog's thick fur.

Tucker opened his eyes and nodded, still struggling to catch his breath. He glanced at her and his eyes darkened. "I think the perp kicked him before running off. And there's blood on his ear where a bullet grazed him." Tucker pulled the dog to him and buried his face in Scout's neck. "He's not supposed to attack without a command," he murmured.

"But he saved our lives," Tara whispered.

Tucker reached out and gave her hand a squeeze. "Yes, I

think he did. We should get moving. He might circle back." Tucker looked deep into the woods where their attacker had fled.

"You're right, but we're not going any farther until I see where you got shot," Tara insisted.

Tucker shook his head. "It's fine. Just a flesh wound."

Tara brushed his hand out of the way and pulled up his shirt, bending closer to inspect his side. Her heart stuttered. "Tucker, I'm not a doctor, but you need to see one. It may be just a flesh wound, but it looks deep. And it's still bleeding. I can only imagine what's in that water we've been swimming in. We don't have anything to use for a clean bandage to even try and dress this wound."

"The number one priority is to find a place to hide until reinforcements get here. My gun's in that swamp now. We don't have time to waste." He struggled to stand but fell backward.

Tara took a hard look at his face. His skin was pale as cotton. He tried to smile, but Tara would have characterized it as a grimace. "I've been in Iraq. This is nothing," he said through gritted teeth. He got to his feet with a grunt, holding his hand out to her. "We need to get under the cover of trees. It's dangerous being out in the open like this."

Tara bypassed his hand and put her arm around his waist. "Lean on me," she said. He put his arm over her shoulder, and they made for the trees. Scout stuck close to Tucker's side. The dog moved with a slight limp, but otherwise Tara was relieved to see that he appeared to be fine.

Tucker's body shivered against her, and she pulled him closer. "Dear God," she whispered. "We need help. Begin mending the damage done to Tucker's body by the bullet. Please send reinforcements to help us."

Tara tamped down the anxiety that whipped through her.

Tucker needed medical help, but they had no supplies out here. Their clothes were soaked with marsh water and would make lousy bandages. She'd have to try and make it back to the SUV for the first-aid kit.

Scout stopped without warning and sniffed the air, his nose pointed in the direction the assailant had disappeared. Against her, Tucker's entire body tensed, and he turned, reaching for his gun that wasn't there. Scout trotted over to a small shrub and stopped. In the watery light something dark stood out against the grass.

"I'll see what it is," Tara said, jogging to the spot where Scout was standing. She sucked in a sharp breath and reached for a gun lying in the grass and mud. Tucker appeared at her side. "He must have lost his weapon!" she said, handing it to him.

Tucker turned it over in his hand. "It's still loaded," he said, engaging the safety. "Maybe something happened in the altercation with Scout." He huffed out a deep breath. "Score one for the good guys," he said, his voice raw with exhaustion.

"Where's the cavalry?" Tara asked. "Your wound is going to get infected. I need to get to the SUV and get the first-aid kit, but I don't want to leave you here."

"Leave *me* here?" Tucker's eyes bulged. "Do you think for one minute I'd let you go traipsing through the marsh by yourself? With the gunman still out there? He could be back at his truck getting more firepower."

Tara perched her hands on her hips. "I can handle myself," she reminded him. "You need medical attention. I can take his gun with me—"

"Listen," Tucker said, looking up. "Do you hear that?"

Tara turned her eyes to the washed-out gray sky. The faint sound of churning helicopter blades broke through the sound of the rain, the noise soon overlapped by the wail of sirens. Relief flooded through her body and almost brought her to her knees. A medevac helicopter came into view. It circled above, finally spotting them. The pilot gave a thumbs-up and the helicopter rose and flew back over the trees.

"He'll find a place to land and report our location so the officers can come straight to us," he murmured.

"Thank You, God," Tara whispered, and pulled Tucker close, putting her arms around him to keep him warm as he shivered.

Within moments officers swarmed the area. Tucker handed the gun over to the officer in charge before paramedics descended on him and began examining his wound. Tara assured the medical personnel she was fine, and stood to the side while they worked on Tucker.

One of the paramedics knelt and began treating the injury to Scout's ear. He caught Tara watching him. "This is just until he gets a thorough examination at Happy Tails, where the K9 officers are treated."

"I'm familiar with that place," Tara said with a smile.

The paramedics stepped away from Tucker. He spotted her and winked. He was lying on a stretcher, and she moved to his side. "Are you okay?"

He nodded. "They gave me something for pain, which I said I didn't need," he growled.

"What's a little gunshot wound?" she said.

"Exactly," he said, slurring the word.

One of the medics stepped closer. "Officer Dawson, if you're ready we're going to transport you to the hospital in the helicopter." He turned to Tara. "You're going to come with us as well. Chief Seever was adamant he wants to give that guy no chance of getting to you again on the highway."

Tucker gave her a goofy grin. "Get ready for a wild ride," he mumbled as his eyes closed.

TWELVE

Mosquitos swarmed around her. Their buzz was like chain-saws and so thick she couldn't see where she was going. Tree branches slashed at her face. Tara ran for her life, but her feet kept sinking knee-deep in mud and muck until she couldn't move another step. She was trapped. He was right behind her! She could hear him calling her name… *Tara! Tara!*

A gentle hand nudged her, and she jolted awake to the sound of a piercing alarm. A nurse scooted past her, an efficient looking woman with gray hair cut short and spiky on top. She turned off the alarm on Tucker's IV drip. "Officer Dawson, you need to get back into bed," she ordered. "You can't just pull the IV out of your arm."

"She was having a nightmare," Tucker said. "I needed to get to her." He peered around the nurse as she pushed him back onto the pillows and he locked eyes with Tara. "Are you okay?"

She nodded. In truth she was shaking all over. She inhaled a deep breath, pulling herself with effort from the harsh images in her nightmare back to Tucker's hospital room.

Her side was still tender, and falling asleep in the brick-hard hospital chair had added a stiff neck to her aches and pains. She twisted and stretched, working the kinks out.

Tara walked to the window. Somewhere out there the monster who was after her was biding his time. A shiver scooted up her spine. Given everything that had happened, she was sure he knew right where she was.

It wouldn't be long before the US Marshals' office had her on a plane out of here and back to their headquarters in Virginia. Would they let Tucker accompany her? She doubted it. Sudden tears erupted and Tara blinked, shoving those feelings back down. She'd come to depend on him, that was all. He'd saved her life more than once, and she would always be grateful to him and consider him a friend. It was best to leave it at that. Her brain tried to remind her of the kiss they'd shared at the bridge, and she silenced those thoughts. It was just the adrenaline from a life and death situation and nothing more.

The day when Platt and his evil cohorts would be behind bars seemed like a fairy tale. Then she could put all of this behind her like yesterday's news and rebuild her life. Alone, she thought, as sadness threatened to choke her.

Tara wondered if Chief Seever would let her return home before she had to leave for Virginia. All she had left of Michael was still there, as well as evidence Michael had hidden for her to find. Dan Cramer knew about it, but now that he'd been shot, she wasn't sure if the marshals were aware of it.

The nurse bustled about for a few minutes, taking Tucker's blood pressure and checking his sutures before giving him a warning look as she left. Tara walked to his bed. "I'm the one who should be asking how you're doing." She smiled. "You look better than you did yesterday."

"That wouldn't take much I'm sure," he chuckled. "I'm sore, and breathing isn't enjoyable because it pulls at the stitches, but that won't stop me. Not after what this guy's put you through."

A sharp knock sounded on the door and Marcus Seever peered around the corner. "The guard out here just said you're setting off alarms trying to escape, Officer Dawson."

"Is that what it's going to take for me to get out of here?" Tucker asked as Marcus stepped into the room.

"I've seen you look better, Tucker. Be thankful they're letting you out today."

Marcus walked over to Tara. "You're a sight for sore eyes too. I can't believe this madman found you on that stretch of highway. I've got Luca working overtime going through all our systems, searching for any way he could be tracking you." Marcus looked at Tucker. "I've ruled out that it's any of our K9 officers. Only you and I knew the route you were taking yesterday."

Tucker scrubbed a hand down his face and sighed. "That confirms what I've believed all along."

Marcus nodded. "Until we figure out how this guy is shadowing you, we have to consider every possibility."

"It would help if we knew who he was," Tara said.

"We know he's involved with Gideon Platt." The chief's eyes glinted. "That weapon you two found yesterday is a ghost gun. We have no way to trace it. And there weren't any prints except yours and Tara's."

"Was his red truck still at the scene?" Tara asked

The chief shook his head. "There was no sign of it. We put out an APB, and it was found in the far corner of a grocery store parking lot outside of Houston. The front grille had extensive damage."

"I'm sure it did, given how hard he rammed us...twice," Tucker said.

"Surveillance cameras in the parking lot show a man exiting the truck and walking off on foot. He had a baseball cap on and was wearing a mask, so his features weren't identifiable. There were no prints anywhere in or on the truck except for those of the owner he stole it from."

Tucker scowled. "He's going to make a mistake, and I plan to be there."

"We did catch a small break," Marcus said. "There were a couple drops of blood on the floorboard of the truck. Maybe from a bullet wound or from Scout's teeth when he attacked. We're going to run it through our database and see if anything turns up."

"Scout earned his kibble yesterday," Tara informed the chief. "If it wasn't for him going after Ski Mask Man, we might not be here now."

The chief nodded. "Scout's one of the best K9 officers we have. He didn't attack on command though. Once this is all over, he may need some retraining."

"How's my partner doing?" Tucker asked.

"He's being checked out at Happy Tails. They sutured that laceration to his ear from the bullet wound. It also appears the perp kicked him in the chest."

Tucker's face turned red. "If I ever get my hands on this guy…"

"There's some bruising," the chief continued, "but Dr. Moore said Scout seems fine. They're keeping him overnight but then he should be ready to return to duty."

"I'm so thankful to hear it. I have a soft spot for that dog," Tara said. She glanced at Tucker and felt heat creep into her cheeks at the warmth in his eyes.

"I'll see you two at headquarters later today once the doctor releases you," Marcus informed Tucker. "I've invited Luca to join us. We're going to brainstorm and see if we can figure out what trick that gunman is using to shadow your movements."

"What's the plan to get us there?" Tucker asked.

"I would've liked an armored tank to transport you," he said with a sigh, "but had to settle for an escort of five patrol cars, with sirens and lights." Tucker's eyebrows hit his hairline. "Covert means haven't helped so far, so I'm erring on the side of protection and firepower."

"Chief," Tara said. He turned, eyebrows raised. "This may be a big ask, but I need to get back to my duplex in Ivy, Texas."

The chief shook his head. "I don't think that's possible. Especially since we don't know how this guy's tailing you. Keeping you safe is the priority right now."

"What's at your place, Tara?" Tucker asked. His eyes were gentle, but she saw the resolve in their depths. He would be a tough sell as well.

She took a deep breath. "There are some of my brother's things there."

Marcus rubbed a hand over his bald head and sighed. "I understand, but I still can't give this a go-ahead. Not with this perp who seems to know what we're doing before we do."

She cleared her throat. "There's also a piece of evidence from Michael I need to retrieve for the authorities." The chief's eyebrows skyrocketed, and Tara rushed on. "I found it a couple weeks ago. I told Dan and he said he'd get it. I planned to give it to him when he arrived to take me to Virginia. Except—" she chewed at her lip "—he never got there, and then this awful nightmare started."

"I'll contact the US Marshals' office," Marcus said. "They'll want that evidence. Until then, for your safety, I can't give the go-ahead for you to return."

"Understood, Chief," Tucker said.

"I'll see you back at headquarters, Dawson. Get back

there in one piece." He shot Tucker a stern look as the door closed behind him.

Tara felt Tucker's eyes on her. He reached up and placed a warm palm against her cheek. "What else is at your place that you need? We'll make sure you get it back."

Kindness softened the intensity of his blue eyes, and Tara swallowed back the sob that tried to escape her throat. "Just some personal items that aren't important to anyone but me. Birthday cards Michael sent during those years I didn't see him, some pictures of the two of us with our parents. I probably should have stored them somewhere safe, but I always wanted them with me." A tear leaked out the corner of her eye, and Tucker brushed it away with his thumb.

"Assignment accepted," he said with a smile. "For the moment, let's just concentrate on keeping you alive."

After the peril of the past few days, Tucker wasn't sure how to react when he and Tara got back to headquarters without incident. He knew his fellow officers would think it odd if he kissed the ground in relief when he walked in, so he made do with handshakes and claps on the back from the rest of the team.

Tucker kept Tara close at his side until Stella wrapped her arms around the woman's shoulders and pulled her away. He was relieved to see Tara laugh at something his fellow officer said, and he appreciated Stella's care and encouragement. She led Tara to a chair beside Tucker's in the team room and got her settled in with a soda and a pack of crackers.

Marcus Seever walked in and headed straight for Tara. "No word yet from the Marshals' office about the evidence at your home."

Luca entered and everyone found a seat. Luca placed his

computer on the table and began typing rapidly. Images appeared on the smart board.

Tucker appreciated Luca's contributions to their team. The IT specialist preferred to be in the background, but his assistance was invaluable, and his expertise was second to none. His dark eyes flicked from the computer screen to the board on the wall, then landed on Tucker. Luca gave him a small smile, which was an exuberant greeting from this quiet, brilliant member of the K9 unit.

Marcus started by giving everyone a rundown of the events of the past several days.

"Are we sure there haven't been any tracking devices on your vehicles?" Katie asked. "Could he have planted them when you weren't aware?"

"I don't see how," Tucker responded. "I checked the electric company van and it was clean. He would have had to know where we were in the first place in order to plant anything after that."

"Are we dealing with a single suspect or more than one?" Stella asked.

"We know there are more than one, right?' Cade said. "The guys we have in custody, plus the man in the blue jeep, who I believe was the same one at the cabin and in the red truck."

Tucker nodded. "We call him Ski Mask Man. The assailant in Galveston doesn't seem like a hired thug. There's a ruthlessness about him. And in that note he left under the windshield wiper he identifies himself as Michael's killer."

"Given that it was a ghost gun he dropped, I think we can all agree he's part of Platt's organization," the chief said.

"Tucker," Luca interjected. "You said there were no tracking devices on the vehicle. Did you double-check things like your shoes, handbags, backpacks?"

Tucker glanced at Tara and nodded. "No bugs anywhere that we could find."

Tara's phone pinged and she jumped. "Sorry, let me silence it." She glanced at the device and frowned, then let out a sharp gasp. Her face flushed red.

"What is it?" Stella asked.

"It's a text from my landlord. He's been trying to reach me. Someone broke into my home. Mr. Garcia got a call that my front door was standing open and went to check on me. The place has been turned upside down…" Her voice dwindled to a whisper.

"Tara, how well was that evidence hidden?" Marcus asked.

Cade's eyes popped. "Evidence?"

Tara nodded. "Yes, something I found a couple weeks ago. A list of some of the key players in Platt's organization. Michael put it where he knew I'd come across it…in between the pages of my Bible at the location of my favorite verse. I notified Dan when I found it but he didn't want me emailing or texting the information to him for security reasons. He said he'd pick it up personally when he met with me next week to discuss some aspects of Platt's trial."

Tucker rubbed his temples. This was intensifying the pounding in his head. "I don't understand it. This doesn't make sense. Why is he tossing your place now? How did he even know about this evidence? Did you tell anyone besides Dan?"

Tara shook her head.

"We know there was a leak," Marcus reminded everyone. "I need to find out who Dan reported it to."

Luca turned his attention to Tara. "Ms. Piper, something's occurred to me. Those dog tags you wear. They were your brother's?"

Tara nodded, reaching up and rubbing her thumb over the smooth plastic surface of the case.

"May I see them, please?" Luca asked.

Tara's brows drew together, confusion shining in her eyes, but she nodded and lifted the chain over her head, passing the dog tags to Luca. "Here you go."

Luca nodded, then turned his attention to the dog tags. The room was so quiet Tucker could hear himself breathing. Every officer sat with their arms crossed on the table, laser focused on the IT expert.

Luca pried open the plastic case and the dog tags swung free. He turned each one over, examining them individually.

"Tara," Luca said, "where did you get these? Who gave them to you after your brother was killed?"

Tara's gaze darted from Luca to Tucker and then back. "Dan Cramer brought them to me. They were in a box with several of Michael's possessions. I guess they were all items that were found in his apartment, where he was shot."

Luca nodded. "There's a tracking device attached to this dog tag," he said, holding the piece of metal and twisting it back and forth.

"What?" Tara, Tucker and the chief said in unison.

Luca nodded. "PlattTech has been experimenting with highly sensitive tracking devices specifically for military use that are super thin and almost invisible. They're made to attach to soldiers' dog tags and can aid in search and rescue if a soldier goes missing, or provide information on troop movements on a battlefield, to name just a couple benefits."

The officers sat in stunned silence, and Tara shook her head. Tucker could see the shock in her eyes, and he reached for her hand, giving her fingers a squeeze.

"Would Michael have been aware this tracking device was on his dog tags?" Stella said.

Luca shook his head. "I doubt it. Tara, did he take them off, leave them lying around where anyone could get to them to attach a tracking device?"

Tara shook her head. "I don't think so. I can't imagine a scenario where he would just take them off, or hand them over to someone and forget about it."

Luca continued. "I believe the tracker was added to the dog tags after Michael's death and given to Tara with his personal effects, with the purpose of using it to track her movements. Gideon Platt's organization has the technology, and he knows she's testifying at his trial."

"That makes sense," Beckett said, "but how did they guarantee she'd wear the dog tags?"

"It was a gamble," Tucker said. "Maybe someone knew the dog tags were important to her. What else was in that box? I wonder if everything has a tracking device on it."

"No wonder they've been in lockstep with every move you've made," Cade said.

"I don't understand." Tara frowned. "I've been in witness protection for over three months. Why has this just started? If he's known where I've been all along, why wait until now to try anything?"

"That's an answer we may not have until we can get our hands on him," Marcus replied. "In the meantime, Luca, can we disconnect the tracking device?"

"Yes." Luca nodded. "I can take care of that."

"Wait." Tara glanced around the table at the officers. "If we know what he's doing, we can lead this guy into a trap."

Tucker's blood pressure spiked. As much as he wanted to see this guy behind bars, he didn't like the sound of setting a trap unless Tara was safely out of the picture.

All the officers began speaking at once, and Marcus elevated the sound of his voice. "Our instructions from the

US Marshals' office are to keep Ms. Piper safe in protective custody until they're able to determine next steps. Not try and trap a member of Platt's organization."

"Until this perp is behind bars, Tara isn't going to be safe," Cade replied. "The man is vicious. He may have other means of locating her we aren't aware of. I think we need to seize this opportunity while we can."

"How can we be sure Tara stays safe?" Tucker asked. "If we can't guarantee that, this doesn't have my vote."

"I have an idea that might work." Tara darted a quick glance at him, and Tucker recognized the determination in her eyes.

"What's your plan?" Stella asked.

"Lead him back to my house. My neighbor on the other side of the duplex won't be there. Mrs. Gray's an older lady and goes north to Maine over the summer to visit her son."

"Once we get everything in place, Tucker, Cade and I can travel there with the dog tags," Stella added.

"I'm going too," Tara announced. Before Seever could object she continued. "I'm the only one who knows where the evidence is hidden."

Marcus sighed in frustration. "I'm not risking Tara getting attacked on the highway again," he stated.

"I have deep reservations about this, but if we're seriously considering it, I can take Tara in the chopper," Tucker suggested. "Stella and Cade can bring the dog tags with them."

"Work out all the details and let me see what you come up with," Marcus said. "I'll consider it. Right now, I'm in Tucker's corner. This could be a big risk."

Tucker's stomach twisted like a snake at the thought of leading that maniac right to Tara. The plan would have to go off without a hitch, because any mistake could be fatal.

THIRTEEN

Tara had a white-knuckle grip on her seat in the police helicopter. The flight to the hospital in the medevac chopper had been a blur. She had been exhausted and hadn't taken her eyes off Tucker the entire trip. She was living this flight today in vivid clarity.

Tucker turned to her with a grin. "Enjoying the view?" His voice sounded hollow coming through the headset directly into her ear.

"Eyes on the controls please, mister," she instructed, and he laughed.

"This is an easy ride," he said. "We'll be there in no time."

Her entire body hummed and tilted with the slight vibration and maneuvering of the chopper. That, and nervous energy made her feel like she was going to jump out of her skin.

The ground zipped beneath them in a blur of browns and greens and the occasional stretch of narrow roadway. Before she knew it, Tucker was notifying the chief they'd be at the landing site in moments.

She spied her house, and it was surprising to see how small it looked tucked in among the trees. Mr. Yost's farm was recognizable in a clearing on the other side of the woods. He mostly kept to himself but he had brought her tomatoes once, she thought fondly.

Tucker maneuvered the helicopter over an open field where several police cars were waiting. The helicopter hovered briefly, then descended straight down like a carnival ride as her stomach climbed to the back of her throat. There was a slight bump as they touched the ground.

For a moment Tara marveled at the skills Tucker had. God had picked the ideal man for the job in her situation.

Tucker removed his headphones and motioned for her to do the same. The sound of the rotor blades wound down, but Tara's body thrummed as if she was still moving.

"Easy as pie," he said. "Wait right there." Tucker jumped down and came around to her side. He reached up and grabbed her around the waist, lowering her to the ground. Warmth shot through her as he held her close, just for a moment, then stepped back.

"Do you have your sea legs under you?" he asked.

The real answer to that question would be no, she thought. His nearness was making her knees wobbly and sending her thoughts into a whirl. All she could do was nod.

They jogged over to Cade, who was waiting at the edge of the field. "Everything's set up at Tara's house. We need to get going so we aren't all standing around in the open," Cade said. "Stella has the dog tags and we don't know how soon he might get here."

"I wish I had Scout with me," Tucker muttered, as they walked through the woods to the road in front of the little duplex Tara called home.

"Scout has big paws to fill," Cade said with a chuckle, "but we have Clove and Shiloh on standby."

Tara heaved a sigh at the sight of the little brick duplex. It had been an ideal home for her. The entrances were at each end of the structure so even though she had a neighbor, it felt like she had the house to herself.

"Are we leaving the K9 SUV in the driveway?" she asked.

"We need the perp to think it's you and Tucker here," Cade explained. "We have motion sensor lights and surveillance cameras at your front and back doors. I found a discreet location in the woods behind the house where I can see the back door, and Stella found a spot across the street where she can keep an eye on the front of the house."

Stella hurried down the walkway toward them. "If you need us, use this radio," she said as she handed it to Tucker. "Or flick the front or back porch lights off and on and we'll come running." Tucker nodded and she pulled the dog tags over her head and gave them to him. "We'll notify you by radio if we spot anything suspicious. Katie and Beckett are hiding farther down the road in either direction. They'll inform us whenever a vehicle goes by."

"Good idea," Tucker agreed. "That way he can't park the vehicle and approach on foot."

"If things go according to plan, we'll nab this guy while you two are sitting on the couch recovering from the past few days," Stella said as she rushed off to get into position.

"We'll get him," Cade said as he had Shiloh headed for their location behind the house.

They got to the front door and Tucker grabbed her arm. "Are you ready? It's going to look like a hurricane went through."

Tara nodded and stepped into the entranceway. It seemed like it had been forever since she'd been here, not just a few days. It was dim with the curtains closed tight, but she could see enough to tell everything was upended—sofa cushions thrown about, lamps in shattered pieces on the floor, plants ripped out of pots and dirt ground into the carpet. Tears burned at the back of her eyes. She didn't have much but what she'd had was now ruined.

With a start she ran to the bedroom. Blankets and sheets were strewn about the room. She pulled open the drawer of her bedside table and pulled out her Bible, thumbing to Jeremiah 29:11. "For I know the thoughts that I think toward you, saith the Lord, thoughts of peace, and not of evil, to give you an expected end." There between the pages was the paper Michael had hidden. Tara rushed back to the living room.

"It's still here!" she exclaimed, and Tucker's eyebrows jumped up.

"I thought for sure he'd find that," he said, taking the paper and securing it in an evidence envelope.

"Wait right here," Tara instructed Tucker as she hurried back to the bedroom. She dropped onto her knees and peered under the bed, dragging out a small metal box. Blowing off dust bunnies, she carried it back to the living room and set it on the kitchen table.

"Is that the treasure box?" Tucker asked.

She nodded. "Cards and photographs. I just need to add this one to it," she said as she walked across the room and picked up a framed photograph from under the coffee table. The glass was cracked and she removed the picture from the frame.

"May I see?" Tucker said, reaching for the photo.

Tara watched as his eyes moved over the photograph. His lips lifted in a smile. "I like the pixie cut you were wearing."

Tara could feel her cheeks turning pink. "I hated it. I thought I looked like a boy. Michael used to tease me and introduce me as his brother."

Tucker cracked up and her tummy flip-flopped. She

didn't think she'd ever tire of the way his eyes crinkled when he laughed.

His blue eyes glittered as they rested on her face. "Tara, I don't care if your hair is long or short. You're beautiful to me, inside and out."

Her heart pounded and the room seemed to shrink until it was just the two of them. Over the blood rushing in her ears, the little voice in her head reminded her that in the next couple of days she'd be on the first plane to Virginia the US Marshals Service could get her on. Tara hated that little voice. She wanted to rush into Tucker's arms and snuggle into his solidness and strength. Now was not the time. There may never be a time, she admitted to herself.

She reached out and took the photo from him and retreated to the table to put distance between them. Her fingers fumbled with the lock on the metal box, which had become blurry and hard to see. She added the photo to the rest of the contents and closed it with a decisive click.

Tucker huffed out a sigh. The waiting had stretched his every nerve to the breaking point. He paced to the bedroom again and pushed the metal blinds apart just enough for him to squint outside. With the lights off in the bedroom, there was nothing to give him away, but he still felt unsettled with the need to be extra cautious.

There was nothing he could see except darkness. The sporadic car or truck that he'd heard whiz by had been of no consequence according to an update from Cade. He could hear Tara in the kitchen heating up a can of soup, but he felt too keyed up to eat anything.

The picture she'd shown him of her and Michael tugged at his heart. Her grin had been big and bright, and her eyes full of trust, not shadowed by the fear and wariness that now often flashed in the green depths.

Tucker moved away from the window and recalled again how pretty she'd looked fretting over her short hair in the photo. He'd wanted to hold her and kiss her and tell her how much he admired her bravery, and that maybe God did put them together in this trial they were going through. Tara had moved away before he could do any of that.

Tucker shook his head and gave himself a mental wallop, reminding himself he didn't want the complication in his life or the vulnerability of caring that deeply for someone ever again. She'd be leaving with a US marshal soon, and he'd never see her after that.

Despite the disappointment he'd felt when she took the photo back and moved away, he was grateful for it. He couldn't afford to become any more attached to her than he already was. Kissing her again would drag his heart that much closer to her.

Tucker peered one last time through the blinds, then walked back to the kitchen. He found Tara ladling chicken noodle soup into bowls, and he pulled out a chair at the kitchen table and dropped into it.

"I wish I could get some food to the officers outside," Tara said.

"They'll be fine. They have granola bars and thermoses. We've all waited in harsher conditions than this." He smiled, blowing on a spoonful of soup.

Tara grabbed crackers out of a box and sprinkled them in her soup, then closed her eyes briefly as she prayed. He watched as she spooned up a bite, brought it to her mouth, then plopped the spoon back into the bowl. She gave him a half smile. "I'm not really hungry. I just needed something to do."

"Not a problem. I've worn a path in the carpet from the living room to the bedroom to go peer out the window," Tucker replied.

"It's getting late. I'm beginning to wonder whether he'll take the bait," Tara said, nibbling on a cracker.

"Maybe." Tucker shrugged, but he had been wondering the same thing. "Everything about this guy has been unpredictable, so I'm hesitant to put him in a box labeled 'my expectations.'"

Tara nodded. "The last thing I want to do is underestimate him."

Tucker stood and took his empty bowl to the sink, rinsing it out and setting it aside to dry. Tara followed him and dumped the contents of her bowl down the drain.

Tucker ran his hands through his hair. He had some questions he needed to ask Tara about Michael, and he hoped she had enough confidence to trust him with the information. He reached out and took her hand, and she let him lead her back to the table. He took a seat next to her.

"You look serious," she said, shifting to tuck a leg underneath her. "You're in your police officer mode now, aren't you?"

Tucker laughed. "I seldom leave my police officer mode. And I do have some questions that I hope you'll answer, and not lose your cool." He gave her a small smile and her eyebrows bunched together. "This killer seems to be cold-blooded in his tactics, but he's deliberate in his attempts to terrorize you." He took a deep breath. "Other than Michael, was there any connection you ever had to Platt's organization, even unknowingly?"

"What?" Tara's eyes shot green sparks. "Absolutely not. How could you think that?" She shoved her chair back to stand, and Tucker grabbed her arm.

"I don't," he assured her. "But this killer is making it personal, and he's toying with you. I'm just trying to figure out why."

Tara's eyes bored into his and after a moment the scowl lines began to soften. She sucked in a deep breath and sat back down.

He enclosed her fingers with his and let his thumb make circles on the back of her hand. "I'm sorry. If there's a connection other than Michael, it must be one none of us are aware of."

"It's a fair question," she admitted. "I think he's on a power trip. He likes the control and keeping us guessing."

"You may be right. What was Michael involved in within Platt's organization?"

"Michael started as a driver," she began. "He would transport the shipments that came into the Houston port. He would drive them across Texas and into Mexico. For a long time, he didn't know what was in the van, but he suspected it was guns." She shook her head and continued. "At the time he was eager to move up in Platt's operation because he knew the money was good. My brother was reliable and didn't ask questions, and soon began to climb the ladder in Platt's corrupt organization."

"So, they started to trust him?" Tucker asked.

"Yes, he worked his way up," she said, making air quotes with her fingers, "to a position similar to a dispatcher. He no longer drove the truck. He coordinated the drivers for when the shipments came in, and assigned the routes they would take. They always varied the routes. Because of this, he always knew when shipments would arrive in port and how they would be transported to their destination."

Tucker leaned forward. "Is that the information he was passing along as an informant?"

Tara shook her head. "Not at first. He knew how it would look to Platt if his shipments started being raided, or if his trucks were stopped en route to Mexico. Michael would be one of the first ones they'd suspect of leaking information. He supplied Evan with random tidbits at first, helping the government build their case, he thought."

Tucker frowned. "I thought you said you overheard Michael tell Evan about a ghost shipment."

"I did." Tara nodded. "Michael was ready to be out from under Platt's operation. He told me he knew he'd have to go into witness protection once he began divulging specific information. Evan said it had been arranged, so Michael started giving details on routes and shipments."

Tara stood and went to the coffeepot, pouring two cups and placing one on the table in front of Tucker. "It wasn't long after he began divulging details that he got the feeling Platt knew about it. That's when he shared all this with me. He wanted me to have the information in case something happened to him."

Tara's eyes watered. She blinked and grabbed her cup, taking a gulp and making a face at the hours-old liquid. "This is awful. I'll make some more." She jumped up and began brewing a fresh pot. Tucker stood and walked over to join her. He leaned a hip against the counter.

"Your world has been turned upside down," he said.

Tara nodded and Tucker's arms went around her. She exhaled deeply, and Tucker felt some of her tension ebb as she relaxed into him.

His radio vibrated and they both jumped. Tucker pulled it from his pocket and put it on speaker.

"Tucker, it's Cade. We've lost contact with Beckett."

Tucker's heart froze.

Cade continued. "I'm taking Shiloh and we're going to

his location to check on him. Stella is still in position across the street. Stay sharp. I have a feeling…" Cade disconnected the call.

He glanced at Tara and her body was rigid. Fear turned her eyes to green fire.

"Tucker," she whispered, "do you smell that?"

"I don't…" He sucked in a breath. Then it hit him.

"Run!" he shouted, grabbing her hand. He lunged for the back door and threw it open. A thunderous explosion silenced everything around him, and her hand was yanked from his grip as he was flung through the air.

FOURTEEN

Tara landed hard on her side, her cheek pressed into the damp grass. It hurt to breathe. With all the strength she could muster, she rolled onto her back and lay there, staring up at the sky. Debris rained down around her. She tried to make her brain work, but there was nothing outside of this moment.

The ringing in her ears was deafening, almost drowning out the crackle of flames and the shouts that began to penetrate her consciousness. *Tucker!* The floodgates opened and panic raced through her. She had to get up. Had to find him.

Tara rolled back onto her side, tears spilling from her eyes at the pain in her ribs. She didn't think she could stand and the world swam in a dizzying spiral when she tried to push herself to her feet.

"Here, let me help you." A warm voice penetrated the cotton in her ears. She was scooped up with ease against a broad chest, her body bouncing as he jogged away from the heat and debris of what used to be her home. The emergency personnel must have arrived. She needed to see Tucker and make sure he was alright. She prayed Cade and the others had escaped the explosion.

She glanced around through burning eyes. Where were the flashing red and blue lights and the emergency workers? She squinted into the darkness. Where were they going? Something seemed wrong. They were in the woods. Ignoring the pain in her ribs, she twisted to look up at the man who was carrying her, and her heart seized.

A sinister bark of laughter sounded in her ear and a voice rasped, "Not who you thought it was, is it?"

Her blood ran cold. Dark eyes glinted with menace through eye holes in his ski mask. The same red and black ski mask the attacker in the marsh had worn. This was the man who'd killed her brother. He'd just blown up her home, and she had no idea how bad Tucker was hurt. Anger, molten and wild, coursed through her and burned up the panic. Fury was the catalyst that pulled her fist back and drove it into his nose. She cringed as she felt the shift of cartilage and bone. He let out a savage cry, and she hauled her arm back again and shoved pointed fingers into his eyes.

She landed in a heap as he cried out like an animal, covering his face with his hands. Even in the dim light she could see blood seeping onto the front of the ski mask. Tara pushed herself up, half crawling half staggering to get to her feet. The earth spun and she reeled, trying to stay upright and get her bearings. Everywhere she looked there were trees. She glanced up. Shouldn't she be able to see smoke or the light from flames? There was nothing, but she couldn't wait.

Tara took off at a run, dodging through the forest, struggling to breathe against the ache in her ribs. She stumbled into a bush and hundreds of sharp little branches were like needles all over her body. She wrestled to maneuver out of the bush, trying to separate herself from the pain.

After a moment she stopped to catch her breath and listen. Indistinct sounds were beginning to seep in through the loud roar in her ears. She didn't hear footsteps running after her but that didn't mean they weren't there. The faint wail of a siren trickled through the darkness, but she couldn't discern the direction it was coming from. Was she going back the way he'd taken her, back to what was left of her home? There was no way to be sure.

She grasped her side and gritted her teeth. Her breath came in pants as she lurched forward, determined this madman would not win. "Dear God," she mumbled, "keep Tucker safe." He had to be okay.

Ahead of her in the darkness she saw the outline of an enormous oak and ducked behind it. She was so tired. It was impossible to take another step. Just for a moment, she'd rest. Tara leaned against the tree and let herself slide to the ground. Every breath sent pain through her body.

The shrill sound of more sirens drifted toward her as if approaching from underwater. Were they coming from her right or left? She sucked in shallow breaths of the heavy, pine scented air, summoning the strength to stand when she heard the muffled sound of something crashing through the underbrush. Trembling overtook her. It was him. He'd seen her.

Tara pressed her body into the tree, ignoring the hard, knobby bark as it pressed into her back. "God, help me," she whispered. Out of her side vision she saw a dark figure lumber past. The assailant stopped about ten feet in front of her and removed his mask. From the back, even in the watery moonlight, his hair looked short and dark. Tara held her breath. If he turned around, he'd see her. He wadded up the mask and appeared to press it to his face. Even with her diminished hearing she could hear him cursing violently.

He plowed forward, and Tara watched as his dark form dwindled and began to vanish in the distance. Where was he going? A crazy idea took root. Maybe she could follow him out of these woods to get to the road. With all her strength she pushed herself up, grinding her teeth to keep from groaning. She tried to keep him in sight, moving from tree to tree in case he turned around. He was moving too fast, and she soon lost sight of him. Her body began to tremble, and she knew she could be going into shock. She had to get out of this forest.

Minutes later the trees began to thin and she stepped into a field. She could make out the dark silhouette of a building ahead and paused. What if he was hiding there? Before she could decide whether to move forward or go back, the roar of an engine broke the silence, followed by the sharp screech of tires on tarmac. The sound began to fade in the distance.

Tara crept forward. This must be the field behind Mr. Yost's house. She moved as fast as she could. He'd have a phone and she could call for help. There were no lights on so he must be in bed. Even though she didn't know him well, Tara knew he wouldn't mind if she woke him for an emergency.

Tara reached his back door and rapped. No lights came on inside the house. If there was movement from within, she couldn't hear it. She knocked again. He was an older man, and might not hear her knocking. Maybe she should go around to the front door and ring the bell. A whimper escaped her lips, and she wrapped her arms around her middle to stop the shivering, not sure she had the strength to make it to the front door.

"One last time," she mumbled. Tara grabbed the door handle and knocked again as hard as she could. Without warning the door opened and she stumbled into the darkness. Her feet tangled over something hard and she pitched forward, landing on her hands and knees with a thud. Excruciating pain in her ribs snaked through her body and she fell flat onto the floor.

Lights zipped and flashed at the edges of her vision. She couldn't pass out. She had to get help. Tara placed her palms on the floor and pushed to stand, but her hand slid in something slick and sticky. She shrieked. Nausea coursed through her, and she crawled and pushed her way forward, desperate to get to her feet, to get away. She came to a sudden stop as her head rammed into the wall and stars blinded Tucker. Pulling herself up and with trembling fingers, she groped along the wall. Her hand passed over a light switch and she turned it on.

Brightness illuminated the room, and she glanced at the smudged red prints her hand had left on the wall. She screamed and spun around. The body of Mr. Yost lay in the doorway, a giant flower-shaped blood splotch covering his chest. Her breath came in short, quick gasps, and her brain decided enough was enough. Tara dropped to the floor like a stone.

Tucker pushed the paramedic away and leveraged himself off the stretcher.

"Sir, we need to transport you to the ER. *Now*," the EMT said. "You've been in an explosion."

"I know that," Tucker growled. As if he could ignore the roaring in his ears and the crushing headache. The strobing red and blue lights of the emergency vehicles were about to make his head explode. "I'm not going anywhere until we locate Tara."

Cade appeared in front of him. "Any sign of her?" Tucker asked, tamping down panic. Her home had detonated under her feet. Her body had rocketed through the air just like his. He didn't believe for a minute she just got up and walked away.

Cade shook his head. "None of the responders said they

noticed her walking around, but it's been chaotic. We've searched the entire yard, just in case she was disoriented and wandered off. No sign of her." He glanced over his shoulder toward the trees. "That means we need to check the woods."

"Let's go," Tucker said, and pushed himself up. He took two steps and listed to the right, grabbing the back of the EMT truck to keep from falling.

"You need to stay here, man," Cade said. "No offense but you'll slow us down."

"I'm going. She trusts me, and I'm not going to let her down. I'll keep up." He gritted his teeth. Eventually the earth would stop spinning. "How's Beckett?" he said.

Cade nodded. "He's fine. He thought he heard something moving through the trees. He flipped his radio to silent and tried to follow the sound but never heard anything else. Given this explosion, the perp probably went right by him."

Stella jogged toward them, Clove at her side. "I have a shirt of Tara's. We're going to track her." Tucker could see the urgency in her eyes. "Time is of the essence, so let's go. Tucker, we'll keep you updated."

"No need," Tucker replied. "I'm coming."

Stella stared at him, as if about to object, before realizing it would do no good. "Try to keep up then. If Clove gets a scent I'm not waiting."

"Understood," Tucker said. He felt disoriented. His body wasn't cooperating with what he was telling it to do. He'd heard and been near plenty of explosions in Iraq but had never been in one. He forced his legs forward, concentrating on staying on his feet.

Tucker knew this gas explosion wasn't an accident. The maniac who'd been shadowing them had to be in the area. The possibility that he'd kidnapped Tara in the chaos afterward was becoming more apparent.

Stella scratched behind her partner's ear. "You ready?" The dog thumped the ground with her tail. Stella held the shirt in front of her partner's nose and Clove leaned in, inhaling deeply. Without warning she put her nose down and trotted over to a spot in the yard, sniffing at the grass.

Stella squatted and Cade played a flashlight over the area. "This must be where she landed," Stella said. "I don't see any blood, just shrapnel and debris."

"Where did she go after that?" Tucker snapped. "I'm sorry," he said, and took several deep breaths, trying to level his heart rate. Every second that passed multiplied the danger Tara was in. But it wouldn't do Tara any good if he lost his cool, and it could even delay them finding her.

Stella placed the shirt in front of Clove's snout and the dog sniffed again. "Clove, find Tara."

Clove lifted her nose to the air, then moved swiftly to the edge of the yard. She stopped at the tree line, then sniffed again. With a sudden movement the Lab lurched forward, cutting a path through the trees that appeared to be angling away from the house. Stella and Cade followed on her heels. Tucker struggled just to keep them in sight. *Tara, what happened? How did you end up this deep in the woods?*

Tucker caught up with them as Clove sniffed around a large bush. He bent over, hands on his knees, and breathed deep. His stomach churned from the exertion and the pounding in his head. His fellow officers' voices seemed to come from a long way off. He straightened back up, still struggling to calm his stomach.

"Tucker, look at this." Cade handed him a piece of cloth.

His lungs tightened. "That's from the pink T-shirt Tara was wearing."

"So she's on foot. But why is she running through the woods? Is he chasing her?" Stella asked.

"She wouldn't stand a chance. She was in an explosion," Cade muttered. "He could have easily overtaken her."

"Tara would have fought him. We've got to keep going," Tucker said, impatience surging through him. He looked up. Through the gaps in the canopy of trees, he could see the sky just beginning to lighten. The sun would be coming up soon, making visibility a little better in the dim woods, but also reminding him of how long Tara had been missing.

Stella held the scrap of pink cloth in front of Clove's snout. The dog's nose twitched, searching for Tara's scent in the air. Clove put her nose down, pushing through the leaves and brush as they ran through the forest. The dog slowed down at a large tree, sniffing at the base, then again lifted her nose to the air.

Stella scanned the ground around the tree. "I don't see anything."

Tucker ran his flashlight over the area. "Over here," he said, crouching over a section of leaf-strewn earth. "Is that blood?"

Cade scanned the area illuminated by the flashlight. Several large dark red drops were splattered on leaves. "Looks like it." He nodded as he pulled an evidence bag from his pocket and carefully placed the leaves inside.

Tucker's heart rate ratcheted up to an alarming level. "Let's go," he urged.

"Clove, find Tara," Stella commanded. Clove took off, Stella and Cade close behind her and Tucker bringing up the rear. The dog ran to the edge of the forest and out into a field, nose down following the scent.

Through his diminished hearing Tucker thought he heard Stella shout "Clove, halt." He pushed harder to catch up to them. Why had they stopped? It became clear the moment he stepped out of the forest into a field. The darkened silhouette of a house was visible on the far side.

Tucker's blood froze in his veins. "If he's got her, he may be holding her captive in there."

"This must be that small farm we saw on the map," Stella said. "I don't like this. If he's in there, then the owner's in danger too.

"We've got to move while the sun's still low. If he takes one look out the window, he'll spot us if we wait much longer. Follow the edge of the field. We'll be harder to see," Cade instructed as they took off. "I'm calling for backup."

Tucker stopped. The pounding in his head and the spike of anxiety at the sight of that dark house had pushed his body over the limit. "I'll catch up," Tucker rasped as he stepped to the side and threw up in a bush. His body shook and splotches of darkness writhed before his eyes. He was on the verge of passing out. He knelt down and placed his forehead on the damp ground, trying to slow his breathing and settle his gut.

The small voice in his head shouted *get up, get up.* He shoved himself to his feet and stumbled forward, working to close the distance to where his partners had paused beside a garden shed. "God, I haven't spoken to You in a long time, but Tara does. I know she's been talking to You. She's been praying for me. If she can't speak right now," his voice choked, "I'm going to stand in the gap for her. God, please keep her safe. Let us find her," he whispered.

FIFTEEN

Tara stood at the sink in Mr. Yost's kitchen, her body shivering despite the scalding water washing the blood from her hands. Tears blurred her vision. The old man's lifeless body was lying fifteen feet away from her with a bullet to the chest. She hadn't known Mr. Yost well. Dan had told her it would be best to keep to herself. But her neighbor had been kind to her. He didn't deserve this. She added Mr. Yost to the list of people she would get justice for because of this madman.

How long had she been out? There was no way to tell, but the darkness outside was fading. An urgent need slid through her to get out of here and back to her house—or what was left of it. She needed to see Tucker and make sure he was alright. Tara prayed to God that he was. He'd be worried about her. There was no doubt he'd be looking for her.

There was a knife set sitting on the counter, and she realized she needed a weapon just in case. The vehicle she'd heard burning rubber earlier must have been Ski Mask Man's, but he could double back. Sliding a carving knife out of the wooden block and drawing in a deep, painful breath, she moved on shaky legs from the kitchen into Mr. Yost's living room. After already slipping and skidding through a crime scene, she didn't want to disturb the evidence further by going out the back door.

Tara hugged her arms around her waist to ease the trembling in her body, then crept forward to the front door. She turned the handle, but the door was still locked. The killer must have broken in the back door, or perhaps Mr. Yost had let him in and then realized who he was dealing with. By then it would have been too late.

Tara pulled the door open and peeked out. She could see the tiniest edge of pink visible on the horizon. It took a moment for her to realize she could hear birds chirping. Her hearing was beginning to return.

She stepped off the porch and stood for a moment to get her bearings. The road in front of Mr. Yost's home led to the main road. If she followed it, she could get back to her house. Light flickered through the trees, and she saw a vehicle approaching. It began to slow down, then the headlights went out as if someone had flipped a switch. The vehicle continued creeping forward before finally coming to a stop. Tara leaned back into the shadows, her heart pounding against her already painful ribs. Was the killer coming back?

Tara didn't wait to find out. She ran around the side of the house and took off through the backyard as fast as she could, slipping in the dew-covered grass.

The silhouette of a man appeared around the side of a backyard shed and began running toward her. Tara shrieked, swerving hard to the left and falling onto her side. The knife flew from her grasp. She clawed her way to her feet and headed for the woods.

"Tara, wait…stop! It's Tucker!"

Tara's heart lurched at the sound of his voice. She skidded to a stop and turned. Tucker's arms flew around her and he jerked her close. Tears sprang to her eyes, and she sagged against him. His heart was pounding out of his chest.

"Thank God you're in one piece," he whispered. He stepped back and placed his hands on her cheeks, letting his eyes move over her face in the weak light. "Are you okay?" She nodded, then darted a glance over her shoulder to the road.

"We can't stay here," she whispered. "I saw a car creeping toward the house. Ski Mask Man may be returning."

"It's okay. That's just a police car. We thought the suspect could be in the house holding you captive. We requested backup but told them to be quiet about it."

Cade and Stella crowded around, and Stella pulled her into a hug. "You've been a hard one to find. We couldn't have done it without Clove." She reached down and scratched behind the dog's ears.

"Thank you, Clove," Tara said.

Tuckers brow creased. "What happened to your knees?" Tara glanced down at the bloodstains on her jeans and bit her lip. She pointed to the house. "It's Mr. Yost." She pulled in a shaky breath. "He's dead. He was shot."

"What!" Cade exclaimed.

"He's lying by the back door. I didn't realize—" Tears began coursing down her cheeks.

"Let's go," Stella said as she and Cade ran toward the house. She could hear Cade barking into his radio to send a crime scene unit and the medical examiner.

Tucker reached out for Tara and she wrapped her arms around his waist, exhaling into the safety and strength of his embrace.

"I thought we'd never find you," he whispered against her ear.

"If I hadn't been so busy trying to get away from that

killer, I'd have left better clues," she said, her voice muffled against his shirt.

Before she realized what was happening, Tucker scooped her up in his arms and a grimace passed over his face.

"Tucker, put me down. You were in the same explosion I was." There was a fine sheen of sweat on his forehead.

He shook his head and continued toward the police cruiser. "You've been through it. We're going to take a ride to your house in the police car. It's time for the paramedics to have a good look at you. I'll notify them we're on our way."

She reached up, placing her palm against his scruffy cheek and turning his face to her. "I didn't know how bad you were hurt, but I knew if you were able, you'd be looking for me."

He smiled at her, his blue eyes filled with warmth. "I can't lose you now, pretty lady."

She nodded and let her head drop against his chest as he carried her to the car. He deposited her into the back seat, then scooted in beside her. It was a short drive, but she almost drifted off against his shoulder before they got there. She felt the vehicle roll to a stop and dragged her eyes open. The sight that greeted her stole the breath from her lungs.

The duplex looked as if a giant had trudged through, stepping on it like a child's toy. Mrs. Gray's unit was reduced to a heap of brick and wood. Tara could see some of the brick and the wooden frame was still standing on her side of the building, but the roof had caved in, her belongings flung all over the yard. The entire structure was water-logged and smoldering. She hoped their landlord would be contacting Mrs. Gray's family right away. Tara clenched her fists. So much destruction, and at least two people dead at the hands of this monster if he was the same one who killed Michael. He had to be stopped.

Tucker lifted her out of the car, carrying her to the medic truck as the emergency personnel came running. They tried to make her lie down on a stretcher and she frowned and shook her head, not having it. She'd just fought off a killer and run through the woods *after* being in an explosion. Tucker smiled at the paramedic. "She's hardheaded. Just do your best."

Tucker moved to the side but didn't let her out of his sight as the medics cleaned and bandaged her cuts and burns. They continued to poke and prod, and when they touched her ribs, she thought she'd catapult off the stretcher.

"I think you might have some fractured ribs, Ms. Piper," the paramedic stated. "You're going to need X-rays."

"Looks like it's a ride to the hospital for you." Tucker smiled. "I'll chauffeur you to the emergency room in the helicopter."

Tara nodded. She let her gaze wander to the debris covering the front yard. Would it be possible to find the metal box with her personal mementos? She gave herself a mental shake. After Mr. Yost's murder and the destruction of Mrs. Gray's home, it seemed a selfish thought. *I'm sorry God, please forgive me. Thank You for sparing Tucker's life and mine.*

"Wait right here," Tucker said.

"I don't think they're going to let me go anywhere." Tara eyed the paramedic, who shook his head.

Tucker chuckled. "Okay, be right back."

He returned a moment later holding the metal box. "I managed to save this. It was lying in the grass right next to me after the explosion. It may even be responsible for this cut on my arm—" he grimaced, pointing to a red gash "—but who can be sure."

Tara's heart flooded with emotion, and she threw her arms around him. Sometimes it seemed he could read her mind. She swallowed back a sob. Her departure with a US marshal was imminent, and she needed to start letting him go. But for now, she held on for just a moment longer.

Tucker paced outside the chief's office. Nervous energy scuttled like fleas under his skin.

Marcus was on the phone with the US Marshals' office and Tucker was sure they were giving him an earful about putting Tara's life in danger with their failed operation to catch the perp. At least they'd gotten the paper Michael had hidden for Tara with the list of names in Platt's organization.

It nagged at Tucker that the killer had known where they were headed even before Stella and Cade got to her house with the dog tags. He pondered the report from the fire marshal about the cause of the explosion. If the perp had been tracking Tara, there was no way he would have had time after they'd arrived to break into Mrs. Gray's side of the duplex, light a candle and turn the gas on, which was what the report indicated.

He rubbed his temples. He'd been trying to remove his emotions from the case and examine it objectively—hard to do given his affection for Tara. Still, it gnawed at him. Every attack since that blue Jeep at the diner had felt personal. It chilled Tucker to the bone to realize that since this maniac was tracking Michael's dog tags, he could have killed Tara months ago. Why had he waited?

Tucker reached down and scratched Scout behind the ears. "What game is this guy playing, Scout?" His partner wagged his tail, almost as happy to be back on duty as Tucker was to have him back.

Tucker resumed his pacing. The heaviness in his heart weighed him down. He was going to have to let Tara go. It wasn't fair to her to be saddled with his issues. Every part of his being didn't want to. How had she gotten so deep under his skin?

The door jerked open, and Marcus stood in the doorway. "Tucker, I saw you pacing through the glass. I'm glad to see Scout with you." He gestured to one of the plastic chairs in front of his desk.

Tucker sat and leaned forward, elbows on his knees. "What's the word?"

"We're taking her to the airport tomorrow," Marcus announced.

Tucker's heart dropped to his stomach. He focused his energy on keeping any emotion off his face. "Do they want me to take her to Virginia?"

The chief shook his head. "There's a US marshal who will be her escort. Now that we've removed the tracking device on the dog tags, they believe it's safe for her to leave."

Tucker jumped up. "Then how do they explain that maniac showing up *ahead of us* in Ivy? This is not a safe move at all." Tucker paced to the door and back. "Is there anything we can do?"

The chief's eyes narrowed. "For starters, Officer Dawson, you need to separate your feelings from this case. It's under the US Marshals' jurisdiction. I may have erred by allowing you to continue. I didn't realize the extent of your attachment to her."

Tucker ground his teeth. "With all due respect, sir, whatever soft spot I may have for her doesn't have anything to do with this. Am I the only one who's concerned that the perp arrived in Ivy *before* we did? Until we figure out who this guy is and how he's shadowing Tara, her life is still at stake."

The chief sighed and ran a hand over his bald head. "I explained that to them. They think she's safer with them. Maybe they're right. We've managed to keep her alive, but barely."

Tucker shook his head. If his blood pressure climbed any higher, he'd pass out. He took a deep breath.

"Luca's removed the tracking device," the chief continued. "We'll get her to the airport tomorrow, and the marshal can get her to Virginia without incident. She should be in a safe location within the week."

"I'd like permission to drive her to the airport, Chief," Tucker stated.

His boss hesitated, chewing at the inside of his cheek. "I don't know—"

"Sir, she trusts me. We've been through a lot together. I'd like to be the one to take her to the airport." His heart threatened to pound right through his ribs.

A knock sounded at the door, and Cade peeked around the corner. "Marcus, we got the results of the blood we found on the leaves. Nothing."

The chief huffed out a sigh. "I was hoping it was the perp's."

"It was," Cade replied. "We took a sample from Tara, and it wasn't a match. She must have nailed him in the nose pretty good. I bet he's got a heck of a shiner now. Whoever this guy is, he's nowhere in the database. Once we capture him, that will be more proof that places him at the scene."

Tucker jerked the ball cap off his head and ran his fingers through his hair. He had the beginnings of a theory. Would they think he was crazy? "I'm going to throw something out there that's been puzzling me. It may be far-fetched."

Marcus nodded and Tucker continued. "When we got to Tara's house and saw the chaos, it wasn't what I expected."

"How so?" Cade frowned. "Everything was upended. Chairs were knocked over, plants were yanked out of pots and dirt was all over the floor—"

"Yes, but no slashed pillows, no tossed dresser drawers, no toppled books. He didn't even touch probable places where someone might hide things. Case in point, Tara's metal treasure box was still under the bed where she kept it. I don't think the perp was looking for anything. I think he was staging it."

"Keep going," Marcus said.

"Whoever did it left the door wide open so it would be noticed. The landlord said he got a call from a neighbor saying the door was ajar and the place looked deserted. Could that have been the perp? I wonder if we ask the landlord if he'll tell us the neighbor said his name was Mr. Yost." The more Tucker spoke it out loud, the more sense it made to him. "I think he wanted us to return to the house. This psycho laid the trap for us."

Cade nodded. "I think Tucker could be right. He set up headquarters at Mr. Yost's. Once the tracking device showed Tara heading to her house, all he had to do was turn on the gas, light the candle in the duplex and hunker down somewhere and wait."

Marcus stood up and paced around the desk. "Tucker, is there a chance Tara knows this man? Could she have any connection to Platt's organization?"

Tucker shook his head. "I don't think so. I wondered about that at the beginning and even brought it up. She said there's no connection other than her brother, Michael. I don't understand why this seems so personal."

"Agreed," Cade stated. "It's like he's trying to terrorize her."

"Given the death of Mr. Yost, we know he's capable of killing someone on the spot. But he's not doing that with Tara. He's enjoying the game," Tucker said. *What kind of monster was this?*

"That would only make sense if there was an underlying motivation," Cade said. "Perhaps this is a way of scaring her into not going through with her testimony and the evidence she has against Platt."

"Not to sound harsh," Marcus responded, "but if he killed her outright, they wouldn't have to worry about her testifying. There's more to it."

Unease slithered up Tucker's back. He grabbed Scout's leash and headed for the door, needing to see Tara to make sure she was okay. "I'll take Scout back to his kennel, then I'm going to the hospital to give Tara an update. May I inform her I'll be driving her to the airport, Chief?"

Marcus nodded, but Tucker read the silent warning in his chief's eyes. The stakes in this case against Gideon Platt were high, and Tucker knew he had to step back and let the US marshals do their job of keeping her safe before, during and after her testimony at the trial. Still, he couldn't shake the tension that coursed through him. The perp they were dealing with was cunning. Did the marshals understand what they were up against?

"Tucker, wait up!" He turned and saw Cade jogging down the hall to catch up. "I'll take Scout so you can get going," he said, reaching for the dog's leash.

"Thanks." Tucker handed over the leather leash and paused. "You're frowning Cade. What's wrong?"

Cade hesitated and bent over to scratch Scout behind the

ears. Tucker paused. His friend and fellow officer didn't often have a problem expressing himself.

"I hope I'm not overstepping, Tucker. I know you've gotten close to Tara. Just don't lose your objectivity, or your sanity. These federal trials can drag out. It may be a long time before you see her again, assuming she even wants that. It might be better if Stella or I took her to the airport."

Tucker felt heat crawl up his neck. "I'm fine. I can handle it." He turned to leave, and Cade reached out and laid a hand on his arm.

"Are you sure?" Cade asked.

Tucker stopped and turned around. *What was with Cade? Where was this coming from?*

"Don't lose your edge, Tucker. That old saying, 'you can't see the forest for the trees,' rings true here, my friend. You need to step back. And that may mean stepping away from Tara."

"Nothing's clouding my vision, Cade," Tucker said, struggling to keep the annoyance out of his voice.

"I know you're not big into praying anymore and I understand why," Cade said. "But we've been attacked from all angles in this case. It's hard to keep a clear head, especially when your heart is involved. Bring God into your decisions. He can help you see the big picture. We all need godly insight right now if we're going to get Tara to safety."

Tucker let out a long, slow sigh. "I've been getting the same message from Tara. It's just been a while."

"It's never too late," Cade said, and clapped him on the shoulder. Tucker nodded, staring after his friend as he led Scout down the hall.

SIXTEEN

Tara glanced once more at the time on her phone. From the minute Tucker had called and said he was smuggling a pizza into her hospital room, her stomach had started growling.

There had been no word from anyone about when she'd be leaving, but she had her few possessions packed in a duffel bag Stella had given her and had been dressed and ready to go for hours. Tara hoped Tucker had good news for her, but she was torn. Would he be able to go with her to Virginia?

She'd woken up this morning to him snoring softly in the chair beside her bed. He hadn't left her all night, even though there was an officer stationed outside her room. When she'd objected and said he should go home and get some sleep, he'd said "Turnabout." Since she'd spent the night in a chair in his hospital room, it was only fair he did the same. Deep down she was relieved. To take her mind off the unknown she'd be facing in the next few days, they'd played double solitaire until she'd started to nod off. Tara sighed. Was he as attached to her as she was to him?

There was a light tap on the door and her heart jumped. "Come in."

A large pizza box materialized around the door followed

by Tucker sporting a bandaged forearm and wearing a big grin on his face.

"What happened to your arm?"

"That gash, courtesy of your metal treasure box, needed stitches. Against my wishes." He grimaced. "Nothing a Band-Aid wouldn't fix."

"Such a tough guy," she chuckled.

"You should have seen the people I had to fend off getting here. Seems everyone wanted pizza instead of their hospital dinner." He placed the pizza on the tray table and reached into a plastic bag for paper plates, napkins and bottles of water.

Tara sat on the edge of the bed, ignoring the throbbing in her ribs, and scooched over to make room for Tucker to sit next to her. He opened the lid and pizza smells mingled in the air. A groan escaped her lips. She started to reach for a slice, and he placed a hand on her arm and handed her a water bottle.

"First, a toast." He smiled.

He was adorable. "I'll play along. What are we toasting?"

"To your long life, Tara Piper, and to your safety. And to friendship."

He tapped his water bottle against hers and smiled. Tara took a long sip of the cool water and came face-to-face with the fact that she didn't just want to be his friend. She wanted more. Much more.

The situation she was in took precedence over what she wanted, though. She could help bring Gideon Platt down and stop huge shipments of illegal guns from being transported around the country. There would be justice for Michael. But her heart ached.

"Hey, what's wrong?" Tucker leaned in close, frown lines creasing his forehead.

"Nothing," she said, concentrating on keeping a smile on her face. "I think I'm just hungry."

"Then here you go," he said, placing a large slice of pizza on a plate and handing it to her.

The spongy crust was topped with tomato sauce, cheese and pepperoni, and her taste buds danced. The hospital food had been unappealing and she'd had no appetite for it. How long had it been since she'd eaten?

"I'm glad you have your appetite back," Tucker said between bites.

"This is delicious," she said, wiping a bit of sauce from her chin with a napkin. "I may go for a second piece."

Tucker reached into the box and handed her another slice.

Tara took a big bite, working up her courage. "So, any news on my departure?"

Tucker grabbed a napkin and wiped his hands, then turned to face her, his expression unreadable. "A marshal will be taking you to Virginia tomorrow."

Tara's stomach went topsy-turvy. "Will you be coming with me?" The question popped out before she could stop it.

Tucker stood and gathered up the plates. He closed the pizza box and set it on a side table. "Leftovers for later if you want," he said over his shoulder.

"You're stalling, Tucker."

He walked over to her and grabbed her hands, pulling her to her feet. "I'll be driving you to the airport." Her heart pounded. This wasn't starting out the way she wanted. "I doubt the marshal will want me to assist him in getting you there."

"But what about what I want? What if I need you there?" She bit the inside of her lip. She wanted to cry. She'd given up her whole life to get justice for Michael and take down Platt. Did she have to give up Tucker as well?

"Tara," Tucker said, warmth shining in his eyes, "you are the strongest person I've ever met."

She huffed out an impatient breath.

Tucker chuckled. "Yes, you are. That marshal doesn't know who he's up against."

"Yes, but neither do we. How do we know that maniac won't show up at the airport?" Tara said. She saw a glint of uncertainty flash in Tucker's eyes. "You're not sure either." She jabbed him in the chest with her finger.

"The marshal won't let anything happen to you, and I'll be there until you get on the plane."

Tara smiled at him. "We make a good team. It's a shame to break us up." Her eyes connected with his deep blue ones. The air around them buzzed with electricity, and the blood whooshed in her ears. She leaned closer. His gaze lingered on her lips, and she held her breath, waiting.

He shook his head and pulled back, putting distance between them. "It's going to be hard enough as it is, Tara." His voice was husky and tight. "I'm not going to make it any harder."

Harder for who…her or him?

"Maybe I can contact you after the trial?" she said.

He reached out and tucked a strand of dark hair behind her ear. "I think it might be better for you to start fresh, leave all of this behind you." She began to shake her head and he continued. "I have problems I'm dealing with. I'd just weigh you down."

Tara gasped. It was like a splash of cold water. He could just walk away from her after everything they'd been through? Her heart broke into small pieces.

"You're right." Her voice caught and she pulled in a long, slow breath. It was an effort, but she managed to plaster a smile on her face. "Tomorrow's a big day then. I think I'm going to get an early night. I'll be fine with Officer Burton outside the door."

Tucker's brow creased and doubt shadowed his eyes, but he finally nodded. "Okay, but don't forget I have my phone on. If you need me, call."

Tara nodded, letting tears flow as the door closed behind him. He was right. She needed to move on. Put all of this trauma behind her. She'd never intended to fall for him, but God had placed him in her life for a reason. Maybe it was just to get her to safety.

Her cell phone buzzed. Tucker. She picked up on the first ring, giving herself a mental jab. Too eager.

"Look, Tara, I'm not comfortable with not being there tonight." She heard him taking deep breaths, then the metal clang of a door closing. His footsteps sounded across pavement, and she guessed he must have taken the stairwell to the hospital parking garage. "I'm going to go home and grab a shower, then I'll be back to stand watch with Officer Burton. Two pairs of eyes are better than one."

Her heart hammered. *Yes, please*, she thought. Instead, she said, "That's kind of you, but you've already done enough. I should be fine—"

The crack of gunfire sounded through the phone. Tucker cried out, then silence.

Tucker heard the blast of gunfire just before a bullet ripped through his ball cap and blew it off his head, singeing his scalp in the process. Adrenaline surged as he dove for cover behind a minivan just as another bullet whistled overhead. It slammed into the metal sign on a concrete pillar behind him and ricocheted into the back windshield of the vehicle, raining a shower of pea-sized safety glass on his already smarting head. He pulled himself up and in a swift movement flicked his hand out from behind the van and back to gauge the shooter's location. Bullets whizzed by.

He dropped to a crouch, held his breath and flew toward the pickup truck next to him. There was more to hide behind and fewer large windows. The bullets had come from the direction of the far elevator, and he moved around the vehicle until he could look over the bed of the truck toward that general area. He scanned the shadows among the smattering of parked cars, looking for movement. There was nothing, not even the gritty sound of footsteps on concrete.

The humidity in the parking garage was stifling. Sweat dripped into his eyes and he swiped at it, rubbing the moisture off his hands and onto his jeans. A quick visual sweep of the ground confirmed his phone was lying near the minivan, way out of reach.

Another blast of gunfire thundered in the confines of the garage, and he jerked as the bullets slammed into a concrete pillar behind him. He brought his gun up, scanned for innocent bystanders and fired shots toward the elevators. Concrete shrapnel flew from the wall but there was no other sound. Where was this guy? Tucker fired again, the blast reverberating off the walls. Nothing. Without knowing where the shooter was, he was just wasting precious ammo.

Tucker knew he needed to call for backup and debated trying to get to his phone before rejecting that idea. He'd be a sitting duck. Banking on Tara was his best bet. She would have heard the blast of gunfire through the phone and would send for help. A jarring thought hit him. What if she came running to his defense herself? He groaned, knowing in his gut that was something she'd do. His heart rate spiked at the thought of it.

Tucker listened again, trying to hear anything of the shooter. He caught the rush of cars cruising along on the street and the blast of a loud pop tune as another vehicle whizzed past. A sudden thought iced his blood. If that lunatic took Tucker out, he could creep up to Tara's room. What if he'd eluded Tucker and was on his way there now? The single officer posted outside her door was no match for this guy. He had to get out of here. And that meant going back the way he'd come.

Tucker narrowed his gaze, letting it zero into the nooks and crannies of the parking garage. Shadows hugged corners where the shooter could be hiding—or he could be crouched behind a car ready to spring if Tucker moved. Tucker's heart thundered. He'd count to ten, then run.

Tucker jerked in a deep breath, then bolted for the door, expecting to hear the blast of a gun at any moment. The only sound was the pounding of his feet echoing through the garage. He shoved on the door and into the stairwell, the fluorescent light glaring after the dimness of the garage. A hulking figure materialized out of the shadows behind him. Two hands violently shoved him to the ground. His gun flew out of his hand and he landed hard. The breath rocketed out of his lungs. Before he could react, a knee ground into the middle of his back and two-hundred-plus pounds pressed him to the concrete.

The attacker chuckled under his breath. "Not the big tough-guy hero now, are you? You're a fool if you think I'd let you have her," he snarled.

This guy was unhinged. Tucker was as sure of that as he was sure he was the only thing standing between this maniac and Tara. Ski Mask Man would kill him, then bolt up the stairs after her. That couldn't happen.

Tucker felt the barrel of a gun rubbing back and forth across the back of his head. More disgusting mind games! White-hot anger flew through him and left behind cold, calculated resolve. His brain checked all emotions at the door and Tucker bucked, twisting his body violently to the left and throwing the perp off him. The sudden movement stunned the killer, and he landed with a thud on his back. He was on his feet again in an instant and came at Tucker, leading with the gun. Tucker jumped up, wheeled around and kicked, slamming his foot into the man's wrist. The creep let out a cry and the gun went airborne.

Ski Mask Man charged, and Tucker jumped out of the way, throwing his leg out and catching the man's foot. The perp stumbled and fell forward onto the stairway, his forehead striking against the corner of a step.

Tucker swiveled around, looking for his gun. A loud yell reverberated off the walls, and the weight of the perp barreled into him, driving Tucker backward. The back of his head connected with the concrete wall and stars flashed in his eyes. His chest heaved as he sucked in the musty air in the stairwell, fighting not to lose consciousness.

The killer grabbed Tucker by the shirt and shoved him against the wall. His face was so close Tucker could see the broken blood vessels in the eyes that glared at him through the ski mask.

"You can't win, Aviation Warrant Officer Dawson." The perp snickered, his lips twisting in a feral smirk. "You aren't good enough. You failed in Iraq and you're gonna fail now." The lunatic started to laugh, and something in Tucker broke.

With a roar Tucker thrust the man's arms away, his hands finding their grip around the perp's neck. The man's cold eyes glittered, and his rancid breath blasted Tucker in the face. Without a thought Tucker placed his thumbs over the killer's windpipe and pressed as hard as he could. The perp choked and sputtered, then brought his arms up between

Tucker's, shoving his hands away from his throat. The man struggled for breath and Tucker grabbed at the ski mask.

The shooter let out a howl and swung his fist, connecting with the side of Tucker's jaw. The K9 officer reeled backward and the perp headed for the stairs. Tucker propelled himself off the wall, taking the steps two at a time and grabbed the attacker's foot, unbalancing him. The man landed on his stomach, crying out and cursing. Ski Mask Man rolled over and kicked Tucker in the knee. An electric current of pain zipped up and down his leg, and Tucker grabbed the rail to stay on his feet.

"You're out of your league," his attacker growled, and scrambled up to the landing. Tucker pushed after him, gritting his teeth at stabbing pain every time he bent his knee.

Ski Mask Man reached for something on the ground and spun around. He had a metal pipe in his hand, and he swung, aiming for his adversary's head. Tucker ducked, then rushed forward, plowing his head into the perp's stomach. The perp flew back into the wall. His head smacked the concrete, and he sank to the floor. His head lolled and his eyes rolled back. Tucker reached for the ski mask just as the clang of a metal door sounded a couple flights above.

Feet pounded down the steps at a run and Tucker glanced up to see Tara's face appear around the corner, a flight above them.

"Tara, stay back!"

The shooter scrambled to his feet and lunged toward her just as Officer Burton appeared behind Tara, gun drawn and aimed at the masked killer.

"Freeze!" Burton shouted.

The perp vaulted over the rail, shoving Tucker into the wall as he bounded down the stairs. He bolted out the door into the garage, the officer on his heels. The wail of sirens sounded through the open door.

Tucker slid down the wall, his breath coming in deep gasps. Tara's arms went around him, and he leaned into her. Her hands moved over his back and his eyelids drooped. She was saying something soft and gentle, and it sounded like *I love you*, but that couldn't be right. He closed his eyes and drifted off.

SEVENTEEN

Tucker woke to muted lights and the sight of Cade smiling at him. He closed his eyes and opened them again. Cade was still there. That wasn't supposed to happen. Where was Tara? He knew she'd been there. He remembered her holding his hand and brushing the hair off his face. He didn't dream that, did he?

"Good to see you awake, buddy," Cade said. "How's the headache?"

Tucker turned his head to the left and right and groaned. Everything rocked like he was on a choppy sea. "Been better," he rasped. "Where's Tara?"

"She's just outside the door," his fellow K9 officer replied. "The marshal who's taking her to the airport is out there speaking with her."

"She's leaving now?" Tucker struggled to sit up, then flopped back down on the bed as the room spun.

"No, take it easy. She's leaving this afternoon, but she told the marshal she wouldn't set foot on the plane until you were mobile, and she was sure you were okay." Cade's eyebrows hitched up. "She acts like she likes you a little."

Tucker felt heat in his face. "Well, why not? I'm likable," he said, his heart twisting. She'd soon be leaving...

The door opened. Tara peeked around the corner, and

he grinned. She had her dark hair pulled into a high po-nytail at the back of her head and her lips were smiling, but he saw the concern lurking in her green eyes. She hurried over to the bed, and Cade stepped back to allow her to move in close.

"Do you have a bad headache?" She frowned, and her lips tweaked to the side.

He shrugged, pushing the button on the bed to sit up straighter. "It hurts, but nothing that would keep a super-hero down." He winked and Tara's cheeks bloomed pink.

"Did you say superhero?" Cade laughed.

"What are you still doing here?" Tucker asked, giving his friend a mock stern glare.

Cade chuckled. "The chief wants to make sure you're okay. I said I'd lay eyes on you and report back. We're meeting at HQ this morning, once you get your discharge papers from this place. The marshal is going to join us so we can fill him in on everything we know about the assailant and what's happened. Officer Burton wasn't able to catch him on foot. It was dark and after the perp got out of the garage and onto the street, he lost him."

Tucker frowned. "He's like a cat with nine lives. How does he keep getting away?"

"We might have caught a break," Cade replied. "There are several sets of prints on that pipe the gunman tried to take your head off with."

"There's got to be something there." Tucker nodded, squinting at the throb that erupted above his eyes but thankful the pain seemed to be easing some.

"You mumbled a couple times that Ski Mask Man knows you," Tara said.

He frowned. *What? He knows me?* Something tugged at his brain, then the dam broke and it came back in a rush. His blood boiled at the memory of that maniac's words. Tucker's failure in Iraq. He knew about that. How? "He doesn't know me, but he knows about me," Tucker ground out.

Cade strode to the door. "Tell us about it when we get back to headquarters. I'm going to track down the nurse and see if we can get you out of here."

Tara reached out and grabbed Tucker's hand. She pressed her palm to his and twined their fingers together. He stared at their joined hands and something about it seemed perfect, not just to his eyes but in his soul. Last night, he'd pushed her away. Is that what he really wanted to do? He had fought to remain emotionally detached from her, but he couldn't deny it now. He was nuts about Tara and he ached for her to stay.

Tucker sighed. It wasn't about what he wanted. It was about what was going to happen. They had to take Gideon Platt's gun smuggling empire down and get this crazed killer behind bars.

"That was a big sigh," she said. "Do you need something for pain?" He rubbed a thumb along the side of her hand and shook his head.

"Now that I'm awake, I've got to stay sharp. Concussion, right?" he asked.

She nodded. "Mild one, and a knee contusion. God was watching over you in that garage. Cade said there were all sorts of bullet holes in the walls." She shivered and he gripped her hand tighter.

"I'm just frustrated that he got the jump on me." Tucker gave himself a mental kick. Every sense should be on high alert, 24/7. "I was preoccupied. That seems to be happening quite a bit when you're around. I wonder if I should take myself off this case, for your safety."

Tara's eyebrows jumped, and she shook her head so hard her ponytail whipped back and forth. "No one is perfect,

Tucker. You can't expect to be. You'll crumble under that stress."

"Lives are at stake. Mainly yours," he said, giving her arm a gentle poke. "I'll relax once this psycho is behind bars. For now, I have to be hypervigilant."

She reached up and brushed his hair back, being careful not to scrape the sensitive bullet-burn area on his scalp. Her touch was better than medicine, and he let his shoulders relax. His eyes roamed over her face, which had become his favorite thing to stare at. "I was having some crazy dreams after that blow to the head," he murmured. "You were telling me you loved me."

Tara's face flushed rose red and she lifted her shoulders in a shrug. "Head injuries can do strange things."

He nodded. "I'm sure that's what it was. It just seemed so real," he said softly as she glanced away.

Her teeth grazed her bottom lip, and the room spun around him. She lifted her hand and placed the back of it against his forehead. "Hmm, no fever. Maybe I should report these hallucinations to the doctor. He may feel more tests are in order."

Tucker laughed, despite the pain that jolted through his skull. "Don't you dare. From now on I'll keep my dreams to myself."

"Good idea." She grinned and her eyes twinkled. She was so pretty it made his heart burst. She stuck her hand out. "Let's shake on that," she said.

"I'd rather do it this way," Tucker murmured, placing his hand at the back of her neck and guiding her face down to him. She placed her soft lips against his, and an explosion of feeling blasted through his body. It wasn't just the kiss. It was the knowledge that she knew about the failures that he thought defined him, and she looked past them to the man she believed him to be—the man he wanted to be for her. Strong, compassionate, reliable.

A soft knock sounded and Tara jumped back, breathing deeply. Tucker struggled to catch his breath. Cade stood in the open doorway. His eyes gleamed, and a smile played around his lips. "I just spoke to the doctor. He'll be in soon to make sure you're ready for discharge, then I'll drive us to headquarters," he announced. Tucker nodded and Cade rocked back and forth on his heels as the silence lengthened.

"Carry on, then." Cade grinned, backing out of the doorway just as a stocky man with short brown hair and a neatly trimmed mustache stepped around him and into the room. He was wearing a blue collared shirt and khaki pants, and his dark eyes zeroed in on Tucker. The man stepped forward with purpose, his hand thrust out before he clasped Tucker's in a firm grip.

"US Marshal Aaron Pruitt. Good to meet you, Officer Dawson." His voice reverberated with authority. Tucker rolled his shoulders and tried to relax, even a little bit, at the thought of this man accompanying Tara to Virginia. He seemed capable, but the killer stalking her was ruthless. Could he trust anyone to keep her safe?

Tara sat on a hard, plaid couch in the airport office they'd been sequestered in. The room was small and dreary, with gray walls and no windows, but it was near the gate where she and Marshal Pruitt would be boarding. He didn't want her waiting in the general boarding area with the other passengers, and Tucker agreed. They would leave the office just prior to getting on the plane.

Though they remained on high alert, Tucker and the marshal kept up a steady stream of conversation. For her part, Tara couldn't focus on any of it. Her head was exploding with a jumble of thoughts, but most of them centered on that kiss with Tucker. She could feel her cheeks pinken up just thinking about it.

Had she made a mistake? Maybe she should have told him he didn't dream it when she said she loved him. It seemed he could read her mind. Had he known she was fibbing? That the depth of her feeling for him had been like a bulldozer, trampling her common sense and leaving an attachment that refused to go away no matter how much she fought it? When she'd been afraid to trust anyone, he'd proven over and over that he was trustworthy, that he cared for her.

Aaron's phone began beeping and as he turned away to take the call, Tucker glanced her way, his eyebrows raised in question. *You okay?* he mouthed. Tara nodded, but inside she wasn't. She wanted to stay right here with him.

Tara had said her goodbyes to the K9 officers at headquarters before leaving for the airport, and she'd had to fight back tears. Each member had begun to feel like family, and she understood why Tucker valued them so much. She'd given Scout an extra-long scratch behind the ears and his head cocked to the side, as if he knew she was leaving but didn't understand why.

Tara knew the team was concerned about her. She'd seen it in their eyes. Marcus had been on the phone several times to the forensic experts in the lab, explaining the urgency in getting the results of the fingerprints found on the pipe. Tara would never forget all their efforts. Without them, she wouldn't be alive today.

Deep down she'd begun feeling a desire of her own to help others the way they had helped her. She hadn't even mentioned it to Tucker because she wasn't sure what he would think, but she'd given some thought to becoming a K9 officer herself once she got through all of this.

She glanced at Tucker and his expression was pensive. He moved over to her and gave her shoulder a gentle squeeze. "Aaron says you'll be in Virginia for a couple days, then they'll be taking you to your new, safe location. He wouldn't even give me a hint where." Tucker huffed out a short laugh. "To be honest, I didn't expect him to. But he seemed pleased with the security you'd have."

Tara bit her lip. "How do they know this killer won't follow me there?"

He held her gaze for a beat. "I think you'll be leaving Ski Mask Man behind here in Houston. Aaron said security is tight where you're concerned. Information will only be given to a very limited number of people, and there's no tracker this time."

Tucker's blue gaze roved over her face as if memorizing every detail. "Where'd that come from?" he said, brushing his thumb over the small scar hidden in her eyebrow.

Tara rubbed at it. "Softball," she said. "I got hit with the ball, but finished the inning before I passed out." She grinned.

"That doesn't surprise me," he chuckled.

She felt heat in her cheeks and said the first thing that popped into her head. "What are you going to do with all your free time once I'm gone?"

Tucker laughed, and his eyes crinkled. Her vision blurred. She blinked back tears at the thought of how much she'd miss those little lines that fanned out from his eyes. He shrugged and twisted his lips to the side, as if pondering his numerous options. "So many exciting things I could do," he said, deadpan, and she jabbed him in the side with her elbow.

"Time to go, Tara," Aaron said, interrupting the moment.

"Of course," she said. Something like pain glimmered in Tucker's eyes. A tight lump formed in her throat, and she tried to swallow it. Aaron led them out of the office and down a short hallway to the boarding area. Her eyes burned. She was going to break down; she could feel it. Up ahead she spotted a restroom on the right.

"Please, I have to run to the ladies' room. I'll be right out," she said, darting off. Tears blurred her vision, and she almost collided with an older lady who was exiting the restroom. She locked herself in a stall and let the tears stream until her breath came in hiccups. Grabbing some tissues she dried her face and took several deep breaths. "God, I need Your strength and Your peace right now," she whispered. "You know the desires of my heart, but I have to finish this journey. Be with me."

She went to the sink and splashed cold water on her face, feeling somewhat revived as the brisk water cooled her skin. The call for her flight sounded over the loudspeaker, and she knew she had to get moving.

Tara glanced around. There were two separate entrances. Which one had she come in? She'd been so upset she hadn't paid any attention. She went with the one closest to her, following behind a woman and her young daughter. The woman stopped once they got outside the door and bent down to tie her daughter's shoelace. Tara shifted to move around the mother who suddenly glanced up at another figure and scooched out of the way. "Excuse me, Officer," the woman said.

Tara started to turn but felt a slight shove from behind and a piercing sting to her shoulder. The world spun. The last thing she heard was a vaguely familiar male voice assuring the young mother he'd get the sick lady to the doctor right away. Then darkness enveloped her.

EIGHTEEN

The call for their flight boomed over the loudspeaker, and Tucker and Aaron looked at each other. *Where was Tara?* Tucker had kept a constant eye on the door, and she hadn't come out. Worry gnawed at his stomach. A woman with short black hair and a chic pantsuit passed by, heading into the ladies' room. Aaron stopped her.

"We're waiting on a friend who's been in there a while, and we're concerned. Can you check on her for us?" Aaron said. Her perfect brows pulled together and he took out his badge. "Nothing underhanded. We're just worried about our friend. Her name's Tara."

"She's about five-six and has long dark hair," Tucker added.

The woman nodded and disappeared behind the door, coming out a moment later. "I'm sorry, I called for Tara but no one responded. There's no one who fits her description. Could she have exited by the other door?"

Tucker's lungs tightened. "Other door?"

"Yes, around the corner." She pointed. "There are two doorways in and out," the woman continued, but Tucker had already taken off at a run, Aaron on his heels.

Tucker skidded to a stop at the other entrance and scanned

the area. Several people hustled by, but there was no sign of Tara.

Aaron's dark brows furrowed. "Could she have had second thoughts and left on her own?" he asked.

Tucker shook his head. "No way." His adrenaline kicked into overdrive, and he spun around, trying to see her among the people moving by.

"There are security cameras everywhere." Aaron whipped out his phone and began dialing. "We have an emergency," he began.

Tucker couldn't stand still. He had to do something. Maybe someone had seen her. He started asking every person who walked by if they'd seen a woman with long dark hair wearing a green T-shirt and jeans.

Aaron appeared next to him. "Let's go. They'll have the video for us in the security office. After my call, deputy marshals from our Houston headquarters will be out to help search."

Tucker nodded, just as a petite, curly haired woman approached, clutching the hand of a young girl. "I heard you asking about a woman with long dark hair."

"Have you seen her?" Tucker said in a rush. "Which way did she go?"

The woman bit her lip. "They went that way," she said, pointing down the hall beyond the boarding area.

"They?" Tucker said abruptly.

The woman eyed them with suspicion. "She wasn't feeling well—she looked like she might pass out. It was a police officer who was helping her."

Tucker's heart seized. *A police officer?*

"I need a description. What did the officer look like?" Aaron asked.

A shadow of fear crossed the woman's face. "The police

are the good guys, and one was trying to help her. Who are you? I shouldn't have said anything," she murmured, beginning to back up.

"No, please," Tucker said. "We're police as well." He and Aaron showed her their badges. "She could be in serious trouble."

The woman sized them up for a moment, then nodded. "He was about your height," she said, pointing to Tucker. "He had short dark hair."

"His eye was purple," her daughter added.

Tucker's heart almost erupted out of his chest. He squatted, face-to-face with the little girl. "The area around the policeman's eye was purple?" he said, rubbing under his own eye with a finger.

The girl nodded. "He did look like he'd been in a fight recently," her mother agreed.

Tucker stood and stared at Aaron. Fear shot through him. "He's got her," he whispered, his mouth almost too dry to get sound out.

"Let's go," Aaron said, pulling away at a run with Tucker on his heels. They arrived at the airport operations center within minutes, and a security officer led them to a room where they could review security camera feeds. Bill Reid, the officer in charge of airport security, pulled up the video footage for the period just prior to Tara entering the restroom.

"Right there!" Tucker pointed to the screen. The image of an officer in a dark blue uniform was visible in the lower left corner, mingling among customers waiting in line at a coffee shop. Aaron, Tucker and Tara appeared, walking up the hallway. The officer spun around so they wouldn't see his face. When Tara darted into the bathroom, he positioned himself with a clear view of either exit.

"He's careful to keep his face turned from the camera," Aaron noted.

"I'm shocked he's out here in public with bruising on his face," Tucker said. "That's easily identifiable. He couldn't walk around the airport with a ski mask on, though."

"He's getting desperate," Aaron said. "This is when he'll make a mistake."

At that moment on the video the young mother and her child stepped out of the restroom. Tara followed close behind. Tucker's heartbeat took off at a sprint as the perp moved quickly toward her. He reached in his pocket, but Tucker couldn't see what was in his hand with the perp's back to them. The mother bent down to tie her daughter's shoelace and the officer moved in closer, jostling Tara.

"Look there." Aaron pointed at the screen. "That movement of his arm. I think he jabbed her with a needle." Almost immediately Tara's body crumpled on-screen. Bile rose from Tucker's gut and he froze, barely able to breathe as the man wrapped his arms around her and pulled her close, half carrying her down a hallway beyond the boarding area.

"Where does that hallway go? Are there cameras outside the door?" Tucker asked. "He's got to have a vehicle of some kind nearby."

Officer Reid pulled up another set of video footage from the outside cameras. In it, the officer slung Tara over his shoulder and ran for a police car on the other side of the parking lot.

Every nerve in Tucker's body was stretched to breaking. He wanted to pound the table with his fist, but Tara's life depended on clear thinking, not temper tantrums. His phone buzzed and he grabbed it. "Dawson," he barked.

"It's Cade. Get back to HQ. We got an ID on the prints. It's a cop named Evan Schenk. Wasn't that Michael's contact? The undercover cop?"

* * *

Tara's eyelids weighed a ton. She pushed them up, squinting as the sunlight blinded her. The gentle swaying of her body was soothing, and she let her eyelids flutter back down. She was so groggy. Nothing was more appealing than drifting back to sleep, but the fog in her brain was beginning to clear. Uneasiness slithered over her. Something wasn't right. Once more she tried to open her eyes. It was a herculean effort to thrust her eyelids up and keep them up. Dizziness made her head spin.

Voices and static that sounded like a police radio hit her ears, then were silenced, replaced by strains from an old country music song. Where was she? Tara tried to sit up but was jerked back down. Her arm was stuck. Tara twisted to see what was wrong and panic shot through her body. Her right wrist was handcuffed to the handle of the armrest on the car door. She was lying on the back seat of a car! The sudden squeal of brakes reverberated in her ears as the vehicle skidded to a stop, and Tara tumbled onto the floor. Pain shot through her shoulder as her arm was almost wrenched out of its socket. The handcuff cut into her wrist, and blood trickled down her arm and onto the seat.

A roar of curse words ricocheted around the interior of the car, and Tara's blood iced. The driver sounded unhinged. He pressed on the gas and the car rocketed forward. Tears flooded her eyes as she tried to push herself back onto the seat. Her arms and legs didn't want to move, and she lay there, cheek resting on the dirty carpet.

The off-key sound of a man singing along to a country tune erupted from the front seat. How did she get here? Wasn't she supposed to be at the airport? Like lightning all the jarring pieces slammed into place, and she swallowed the scream that almost exploded full force. They'd been getting ready to board. She'd gone to the ladies' room. The mother and her daughter. The sharp sting in her shoulder, and then nothing.

It was him, Michael's killer. Ski Mask Man. He had her. Fear, like a living thing, threatened to crush her. Did Tucker have any idea where to look for her? Was he already on his way, or was she on her own? Tara sucked in deep breaths, speaking peace over herself. God was with her. She wasn't alone. He was her strength and her ever-present help in her time of need. "God, please help me, please help me," she whispered under her breath.

She couldn't get justice for Michael by cowering on the floorboard of the car. She pulled herself back onto the seat, and lay still, panting while the world spun. Ski Mask Man didn't seem to be paying attention to her. That was good.

She had to be prepared to fight this lunatic and stay alive until Tucker arrived. Tara closed her eyes, forcing her foggy brain to work out a plan. If she pretended to be unconscious when they arrived at their destination, he'd have to undo the handcuff to get her out of the car. He'd let his guard down, and then she'd make a run for it.

How long had she been out? The sun was still shining. A quick peep and she guessed it was midafternoon. She would have been missing now for a couple hours. Fear washed over her again, and she willed her mind beyond it. There were three things she knew for certain. God was with her. He'd brought Tucker into her life. And Tucker was searching for her.

She closed her eyes, trying to muster her strength. Tires hummed over pavement as the car traveled farther away from the Houston airport. The sharp smell of sweat and the cloying tropical scent of an air freshener combined to make her stomach roll.

"Hey! You awake back there?" he yelled.

Adrenaline raced through her, but she kept her eyes closed and willed herself to breathe in a deep steady rhythm. If she hadn't been cuffed to the car door she would have tried to overpower him. On second thought, it was unlikely she'd do anything but cause them to crash as he sped down the highway. She needed to wait for the perfect moment.

"Enjoy your sleep, Tara Piper. You know what they say about payback." He seemed to know her. If only she could remember him, she could use that element of surprise against him. A shrouded memory tried to surface, but it disappeared in her muddled brain like a puff of smoke.

Tucker would have seen what happened to her. There were security cameras all over the airport. She believed he'd be searching for her but if he didn't get here in time, she had to be prepared.

The car began to slow down. Tara made her body go limp and let herself slide on the seat as he made a sharp turn. They bumped along, and she guessed they were on a gravel or dirt road. She took a peek and her heart sank. She could see the tops of tall trees. They were in some kind of forest. How would Tucker find her deep in the woods?

The vehicle continued to bounce along, going farther into the trees and away from the main road. Her heart pounded hard against her ribs, and she took deep calming breaths, clearing her mind of all thoughts but the goal. Surprise him, overpower him and run as fast as she could. *Dear God, please give me strength.*

The car lurched to a stop, and she managed to roll like a limp doll with the movements of the car. Tension zipped like a hot wire through her body.

His door slammed, and she could hear feet crunching on gravel as he came around the car and opened the back door.

An instinctive grunt slipped out as she was pulled along the seat, her body half out the door with her wrist still attached to the arm rest. He jabbed her hard in the arm. "Get up," he snarled.

Tara groaned and lolled her head to the side, doing her best unconscious impersonation. He growled under his breath and she heard keys jingle, then her arm dropped free from the armrest. She let it dangle, staying motionless as best she could and praying he believed she was still out.

Without warning he grabbed her arm and yanked her out of the car. She crumpled on the ground and lay there, unmoving. He toed her side with his boot in the sensitive area of her ribs and another grunt escaped her lips.

"I have a way to get you up and moving," he growled. The moment he jerked the front passenger door open and leaned inside the car, Tara scrambled to her feet and took off, not daring to look back. Her muscles were loose and weak, and she struggled to stay on her feet as she bolted as fast as she could into the trees. She heard an angry roar, and his feet pounded behind her.

"Get back here!" he bellowed.

Tara had no thought for where she was going other than to get away and back to the main road. She darted a quick look around. The sun was still high enough that only brief patches of sunlight filtered through the thick canopy of evergreens onto the forest floor. The farther she ran, the dimmer it got. Her gaze darted about as she looked for a place to hide.

The blood whooshed in her ears as she ran, but she could still hear his footfalls behind her. *Keep going, keep going!* She needed a weapon and would have given anything to have Tucker's Glock.

Tall pines flew by in a blur, and she prayed she wouldn't

slip on their slick, brown needles. Tara pushed harder, fighting against pain and exhaustion. A sudden searing jolt stabbed her in the back and she screamed. Electricity ricocheted from head to toe, and her body began to spasm. She fell to the ground, facedown in the spikey pine needles.

Tara could hear him stomping closer. She wanted to get up, get away, but her limbs felt like spaghetti. Had she been shot?

She heard a tsking sound. "Poor Tara, deciding to take a nosedive in the pine needles. You don't need these anymore," he announced as he bent over and jerked the darts from the taser gun out of her back. Tara screamed at the sudden fiery pain and tears coursed down her cheeks.

"Did that smart?" he hissed. Something in his tone gave her the creeps, and then it began to click into place. She recognized that voice but her brain struggled to put the pieces together. He jerked her up and she sucked in a horrified breath as she came face-to-face with the killer—her brother's police contact, Evan Schenk.

NINETEEN

Adrenaline surged through Tucker's body like a living thing. How could he have been so blind? Of course there would be some police officers in Gideon Platt's back pocket. He'd gone so far as to suspect members of his own unit but hadn't thought further out than that. That had to be how Evan knew of Tucker's past. He should have considered it, especially knowing how closely Evan had worked with Michael. Platt's tentacles, and the people on his payroll, went deep.

Tara had mentioned Evan wanting to spend time with her, and she'd nipped it in the bud. Was that why he was stalking her, toying with her? Because she'd rejected him? Why hadn't Tucker seen that? He mentally kicked himself again and acid gushed in his stomach. He'd failed her. Just like he'd failed Deacon.

"Stop torturing yourself, Tucker." Stella's voice behind him sounded hollow in the hangar of the Houston Air Support facility.

"Why didn't I see it, Stella?" He stalked to the door and back as impatience surged. How long did it take to get the chopper on the dolly and out of the hangar?

"Why didn't any of us see it? We're in law enforcement.

The last thing any of us wanted to see was this. He was Michael's contact. He was supposed to be a good guy," she said.

"It's no excuse," Tucker snapped.

"Tucker, you aren't perfect. And sometimes the most obvious thing can be right under your nose and you're blind to it."

Frustration coursed through him. "Now you've boarded the train full of people telling me I'm too emotionally involved to see the big picture?"

"It's obvious how much you care about her." Stella's eyebrows rose. "In fact, I'd probably use the L word."

Tucker met her brown-eyed gaze for a moment before he looked away.

"All of us missed the connection. But Tara needs clear heads right now, not blame games," she stated.

Tucker nodded. "You're right," he said, with a sharp thrust of his fingers through his hair.

Cade approached at a run. "You have coordinates for his police car?" Tucker asked.

"Got 'em. He's heading into the Piney Woods. He must have a cabin or a hideout there. I bet he didn't think we'd get an ID on him so fast. I'll give you a real-time location once you're in the air. We'll track him right to his door."

"Got it. Tell Aaron if he's riding with me to come on. I'm out," Tucker said, heading for the exit.

Cade caught up to him. "See you there. Keep the faith, buddy."

Tucker nodded as he and Scout rushed out the hangar door to the waiting chopper.

Tara's eyes prowled around the kitchen of the grungy little house, memorizing her surroundings. She was seated on a rock-hard wooden chair at the kitchen table, and her hands were cuffed behind her back. They were going numb, but she continued to surreptitiously flex her arm and leg muscles. If an opportunity presented itself, she couldn't afford to be too stiff to move.

She'd heard the sound of the police radio in his car and knew there would be a GPS tracking system in it. If Tucker had figured out who he was, the police would know where to locate his car and the cavalry would be on the way. She just had to stay alive until they arrived.

Evan had positioned himself across from her, the gun lying on the table next to him and pointed straight at her. He typed something on his phone, then shoved his chair back with a scrape across the linoleum. Tara's mouth turned to a desert as he walked around the table and placed a hand on her shoulder, his fingers flexing at her neck. He bent down and leaned in so close to her face she could feel his stubble rub against her cheek. Her stomach rolled. His other arm whipped around, holding his phone out in front of them. "Smile for the camera." Before she could react, he'd snapped a picture. He punched phone keys with his thumbs and sat down with a grin.

How had she never discerned the unhinged gleam in Evan's eyes before? Why had she not suspected it was him? Searing anger flowed through her. Michael had trusted him. Evan had betrayed Michael and then killed him. Determination clenched her fists. She was going to take him down. Getting out of this cabin was key.

He'd shuttered the blinds, but sunlight sneaked in through the slats, giving her enough light to try and peer into the corners. If she could get loose, there had to be a weapon somewhere. Maybe a kitchen knife or a frying pan?

"What's got you so serious?" Evan said, sneering. "Trying to figure a way out? If I were you, I wouldn't waste any brain power on that."

"Thanks for the advice," she snapped.

He smiled and let his hand rest on the gun, fingering the trigger.

Tara's heart rate sprinted to an alarming pace, and she struggled to keep her expression neutral. She would not let him see he was getting to her. If she got him talking, that could buy her some time. A sudden thought sent fear lurching through her veins. What if he'd done something to deactivate the tracking on the police car? If Tucker was trying to find her, it would be like looking for a needle in a haystack in these woods. She pulled in a long, deep breath. *Focus on what you can control. Get him talking.*

"How did you know we were going to be at the airport? I'm sure you noticed we deactivated the tracking from Michael's dog tags."

His dark eyes glinted. "Money talks. Especially when you have Platt's funds at your disposal."

Tara's stomach lurched. "You mean someone on the K9 team?"

He snorted. "No. They're all Goody-Two-shoes. I have contacts in the building who keep their ears and eyes open. They get paid a lot of cash to do it," he said as he took his hand off the gun and rubbed his thumb back and forth over the tips of his fingers. "One of my contacts heard a US marshal was there and figured I'd like to know. He was right. After that it was just a matter of discreetly tailing you to the airport. I'm in a cop car. I bet they didn't look twice. I followed you in at the law enforcement entrance and hung out until the opportunity presented itself. It always does." He grinned, ice in his eyes. It chilled Tara to her core.

"Why would you do this, Evan? Gideon Platt smuggles guns into the country that kill so many innocent people."

He jerked forward, his mouth twisted in a snarl. "Spare me. Being a cop is long hours and not a lot of pay. Putting your life on the line every day. I was never gonna get ahead that way. I hooked up with Platt and made myself invaluable. I helped ferret out people on his payroll who weren't as loyal as they should be." He smirked. "Platt figured Michael had spilled his guts to you. After the boss ordered you taken out and his goons couldn't get anything right, I told him I'd handle it. Just like I took care of your brother, the traitor." He lifted his gaze to the ceiling as if remembering a fond memory. "Michael was so relieved to see me when I arrived. Then when his back was turned—" he lifted the gun and pointed it toward her head "—bam!" he said.

Tara could feel the blood seep from her face, and she dug her nails into her palms. She wouldn't cry. *Focus. Keep him talking.*

"It was a stroke of brilliance when I hid that tracker between Michael's dog tags. I figured it might come in handy. Afterward, when I saw you wearing them at his funeral, I knew I'd struck gold." He glowered at her. "It stuck in my craw that you treated me like I was beneath you. This way, I got to have a little fun. And you're gonna pay for this," he said, pointing to the purple swelling under his eyes.

His phone pinged and he glanced at it. "The time has come." A cunning smile creased his features. "Platt got that cute photo of us and deposited half the money in my account. To get the balance due, I just have to finish the job."

He picked up the gun, running his fingers over it, and Tara's stomach dropped to her toes.

She licked her lips. "I have more questions about how you accomplished all this."

He leaned back and studied her for a moment, then shrugged. "I've been paid. Ask away."

"Can I have some water first? My throat is parched." She bit her lips together trying to look as harmless as she could. He glared at her, but went to the kitchen cabinet, grabbed a glass and filled it with tap water, then brought it over and held it to her lips. That wouldn't do—she needed her hands free.

Tara attempted to drink while he held it, tipping the glass on purpose and spilling it down her shirt and on his hand. He growled. "You're so clumsy."

"Can I please hold it myself? It's just a glass of water. I'm not asking you to give me a meat cleaver." She gave him a wide-eyed innocent stare and held her breath.

Evan scowled at her but unlocked the cuff from her left wrist and handed her the glass. She took a small sip, then another. He turned to walk back to his chair and Tara arced her right arm across her chest, then swung with all her might. The handcuff still dangling from her right wrist caught him in the temple with the smack of metal hitting bone. He let out a jarring cry and grabbed his head, stumbling to his knees. Blood leaked through his fingers.

Tara turned and bolted for the front door. Her fingers shook as she fumbled with the lock, then all at once she was outside and free. *Woods or dirt road?* If she could make it to the main road, it would be easier for Tucker to find her. She sprinted down the rutted drive, legs pumping and her heart stuck in her throat.

Tucker held a death grip on the helicopter controls. Sweat clung to his brow and trickled down his back. Déjà vu was like a snake, encircling him and squeezing his chest tight. He was in a chopper, once more racing to save the life of someone he cared about. Who was he kidding? Stella was right. *Cared* was a weak word compared to what he felt. He loved Tara. She was everything to him. And he had a wishful thought she might love him too, flaws and all.

"God," he whispered under his breath, "Tara wants me to find my way back to You. To let You take my hand and lead me through the valleys. I'm reaching for Your hand now. I can't lose her. Please keep her safe. Let me get to her in time."

His eyes roamed over the control panel. Based on the coordinates they were getting close. The ground zipped by below, densely packed with lush, green pines. A ribbon of road wound through the trees, and he suspected this was the route Evan had driven on. Tucker began scanning for an open field to land.

"Tucker!" Aaron's voice burst forth through the headset, and he pointed out the curved windshield to a small figure barreling out of a house.

"It's Tara!" Tucker said, relief flooding him. *Thank You, God, she's still alive.* "Look, there's the hideout," he said. His stomach sank to his feet as a man stumbled out of the house and looked up, then pointed his gun directly at the chopper and fired.

TWENTY

Tara's breath lurched in and out of her lungs. Over the deafening roar of blood in her ears, she heard the thumping of helicopter rotors. *Tucker!* Hope surged as she skidded to a stop and looked up, shielding her eyes against the glare of the setting sun. She began waving her arms back and forth and jumping up and down. Did he see her?

A movement caught her eye, and she looked in horror as Evan bolted out the door. He pointed his gun at the chopper, and the explosion of gunfire echoed through the woods. Tara shrieked. His head jerked in her direction, and he came charging like a bull. She took off, her feet pounding hard on the gravel road. The blast of a gun reverberated, and she tensed, expecting the searing pain of a bullet entering her flesh, but there was nothing. She must be out of range, but not for long if the fury in his face was anything to go by.

The crack of gunfire sounded again and Tara jerked. She was an easy target out in the open. The road curved and she veered into the trees, hoping to find cover before he realized she'd left the road.

The setting sun created dappled patterns across the forest floor that played with her vision as she flew past. She mistook a tree root for a shadow and plummeted to the ground. With a grunt she clawed her way to her feet and continued running. Her knee throbbed but she ignored it. Tucker was here. Somewhere.

Tara darted behind a large tree to catch her breath and listen for the chopper. She'd heard the thumping blades in the distance but couldn't hear it now. Tucker must have seen her, and he wouldn't leave. Maybe he'd landed the bird and was looking for her. She pushed off from the tree.

A gun blast shattered the hush of the forest. The bullet whizzed past and slammed into a tree behind her, sending bark flying. He was catching up! Tara zigzagged through the undergrowth and among the pines, trying her best to be a difficult target. She prayed Tucker had pinpointed her location.

Another gunshot echoed and the bullet hissed by, mere feet from Tara's face. *Keep going, keep going.*

The trees thinned and she flew out of the forest into a clearing and slowed to a stop, staring in disbelief. She'd reached a dead end, some kind of cliff edge that dropped off.

Tara ran across the grassy slope to the edge, prepared to go over the precipice if she had to. She leaned forward, peeking over as panic raced through her. It was farther down than she thought it would be. Bushes and a few spindly trees clung to the rocky face. It wasn't a sheer drop off but was steep enough that one wrong step would send her tumbling to the bottom in a hurry. But if she could manage to stand up after landing on those rocks, she'd find a way to keep going.

Heavy footsteps plowed through the undergrowth, and she whirled around. Evan appeared out of the trees.

"No! Stay back!" she yelled. The smile that morphed across his face sent fear slamming through her veins. The gun was pointed at her chest and he began walking toward her, one slow step at a time.

* * *

The blast of gunfire sounded through the woods, and Tucker flinched and skidded to a stop. "Scout, halt," he commanded as Aaron caught up to them.

"That way." Tucker pointed through the trees. "C'mon, we have to keep going. Scout, find Tara." His partner took off with Tucker at his heels. *Hang on, Tara. I'm coming.*

"I think we're getting close," Aaron said through deep breaths.

Close, yes, Tucker thought. But when you were dealing with a maniac firing bullets, close was like a thousand miles. Anxiety and frustration wrestled in his stomach. This was taking too long! They'd found a large enough field to land in, an answer to prayer, but it took time to land a helicopter. Tucker didn't like the head start Evan had on them.

Two more cracks of gunfire sounded, and fear shot through him. His head, pounding from the concussion, had intensified to the point he was seeing stars, but Tucker pumped his legs harder, flying through the trees. His toe caught a rock and he hit the ground, rolled and kept going. If Evan was still shooting, Tara was still alive. *Please God!*

"Tucker," Aaron shouted, "let's separate. You follow Scout and I'll circle to the other side. We'll flank him. He can't take out both of us at the same time."

Tucker held out his arm and flashed a thumbs-up, not breaking stride. After a moment the trees began to thin and the hair on the back of his neck stood up. Was that Tara's voice? "Scout, drop back," he commanded. The dog stopped, nose pointed toward what looked like a clearing in the distance, then fell in behind Tucker.

Tucker moved in quick, low sprints, moving with stealth over the pine needles. They were like a deep carpet, masking his footsteps.

Evan's back was to Tucker and he couldn't see his face, but the man's tone dripped with menace. The killer was moving toward Tara, gun pointed at her chest and almost close enough to reach out and snatch her hand. Terror and determination fought in Tara's eyes, and his heart nose-dived to his toes as he noticed her slight backward step toward the edge of what had to be a cliff. How steep was that drop-off? What was below it?

He dropped to a crouch, leveling his gun at Evan's head. Anything less and he knew Evan could still try to shoot Tara. Tucker braced to fire his weapon when her gaze suddenly shifted toward him. Their eyes met and held for a beat, then two.

Evan noticed. His head jerked in Tucker's direction. With a roar, Evan spun back to Tara and fired. But the assassin was too late. She'd already jumped over the ledge.

Eyes blazing, Evan charged across the clearing toward Tucker, arm raised and firing his weapon. Tucker dove to the ground and rolled behind a tree as bullets shattered the bark and sent it flying. He twisted to a squat and pivoted around the trunk, leading with the Glock. Evan raised his arm to fire again, and Tucker took aim. Before Tucker could pull the trigger, a shot thundered from across the clearing.

The gun dropped from Evan's hand. He fell face forward to the ground with a thud, but Tucker was already up and running, Scout at his heels. He looked over the edge and his whole world went sideways. Tara lay unmoving, her foot bent at an odd angle and blood on the ground beneath her head. "Dear God, please, please, please," he whispered. Leveraging himself over the edge, he skidded and slid to the bottom, getting to Tara in moments.

Her chest rose and fell in a shallow, steady rhythm. "Thank You, God, she's breathing," he whispered. He reached out a shaky hand and felt for a pulse. It was strong and he thought he'd pass out with relief. "Tara, can you hear me?"

Her eyelids fluttered and she tried to turn her head in his direction, then winced. Tucker grabbed her hand. "Don't move, stay still. I'll shift to where you can see me."

"Tucker," Aaron shouted over the edge, "I've called 911. A medevac chopper's on the way."

Tears slipped from her eyes. "My ankle. It hurts."

"I'm sorry you're in pain," he choked out. "We'll get you to a doctor soon."

Her lips curved in a slight smile. "What are your eyes watering for?"

Tucker shook his head, unable to get the words out past the giant lump in his throat.

Her grip tightened around his hand. "I was praying I'd see your face when I opened my eyes."

"If I have my way, you'll be seeing a lot of my face," he said with a wink.

"Promise?" she whispered, and he nodded. The impish gleam that he loved was back in her eyes. "Then seal it with a kiss."

Tucker happily obliged.

Four months later

Tara glanced out the window for the tenth time, doing a little happy dance when she saw Tucker pull into the parking lot of her apartment building. He climbed out of the SUV and she sighed. Even from a distance, just the sight of him made her heart sing.

The vehicle's back door sprang open, and Scout jumped out, shiny Mylar balloons attached to his collar. He looked at Tucker expectantly, tail wagging, and Tucker reached down and scratched his partner behind the ears. Tucker leaned back into the vehicle, pulled out a bouquet of flowers and glanced up at her window. His face creased in a smile when he saw her and he tossed a wave in her direction, then headed to the entrance of the building.

Tara took a deep breath. She'd just gotten off the phone with Marcus and had the most exciting news. She hoped Tucker thought so too.

Several knocks sounded on the door, and she darted to open it, flinging herself into his arms and pulling him into the apartment. His arms wrapped around her and held her to him. He nuzzled her neck, giving her a soft kiss behind her ear, then a tight squeeze before pulling away.

"You're shining like a new penny, as my grandmother would say," he laughed.

Tara grinned. "Are those for me?" she said, reaching for the bouquet of hot pink, yellow and orange Gerbera daisies.

"No, I just thought they complemented my uniform," he chuckled. She rolled her eyes and shoved him in the shoulder before grabbing the flowers and taking them to the kitchen.

"What's the occasion that calls for balloons and flowers?" she asked as she arranged the daisies.

He dropped onto a kitchen chair. "We're celebrating you getting that boot off your ankle, and the end of the trial."

She grinned, happier than she could ever remember being. "Free is the word for the day," she announced. "Free of that ankle boot, free from the trial and everything associated with Gideon Platt." She twirled around and he reached out and grabbed her hand, pulling her onto his lap. She placed her hands on his shoulders and stared into his deep blue eyes. With a finger she gently traced the laugh lines that fanned out from the corner of his right eye and giggled when it made him squint.

"I'm so proud of how you kept your cool during that trial," he said. "Everything you went through to get there and get justice for your brother."

Tara nodded. "I used to have nightmares that I'd be on the witness stand and unable to get the words out about Platt's gun smuggling operation. He'd stare at me with this evil grin as I froze up. Then he would go free because of my failure."

"Yes, well, that didn't happen." Tucker squeezed her hand. "His company is in shambles and headed for bankruptcy, and his government contracts have been canceled." He shook his head. "And then he tried to help himself by turning on all the law enforcement and government officials who were on his arms trafficking payroll. That backfired because they had already turned on him. I guess he didn't appreciate he was the big fish everyone was after. He and Evan will be behind bars for the rest of their lives." Tucker traced the edge of her jaw with a gentle finger. "I hope you realize how proud Michael would be of you."

Tara nodded, tears shimmering in her eyes. "I wouldn't have been able to do it without you and Scout. You know, I think he would have approved of you," she said, and leaned forward, placing a soft kiss on his mouth. His arms tightened around her as he deepened the kiss. She pulled back and smiled. "But first, I have big news." She jumped up, too excited to hold on to the secret any longer.

Tucker stared expectantly and she licked her lips. "I just got off the phone with Marcus. It's official. I'm going to begin training with the police academy. Then I'll begin specialized K9 training. Marcus wants me on the team." Tara clapped her hands and held her breath, waiting for his reaction.

Tucker jumped up, grabbing her and swinging her around before depositing her back on her feet. Scout gave several excited barks, and Tara placed her hand in front of his nose so he could give it a lick. Tucker took her face in his hands, and warmth zipped through her at the love shining from his eyes.

"You know what that means?" he asked.

It meant so many wonderful things to her, but she was curious what he thought. "Tell me." She smiled.

His eyes gleamed. "There will be three officers in the family."

She blinked. "Three?"

"Yes. Scout, me…and you." He reached into his pocket and pulled out a little black velvet box, lifting the lid to reveal a sparkling diamond ring. "God brought us together. I think He meant for it to be forever. That's how long I'll love you, Tara."

Tara brought her hands to her mouth and gasped.

Tucker's eyes crinkled as he smiled at her. "Tara Piper, will you marry me?"

"Yes, yes, yes!" she squealed. "I love you so much, Tucker." She flung her arms around him and he kissed her. Excitement bubbled in her veins and her heart thudded against his. As he wrapped his arms around her and pulled her even closer, Tara could only marvel at how God could take both their lives and bring such beauty from ashes.

* * * * *

Dear Reader,

I hope you enjoyed Tara, Tucker and Scout's story. I'm so grateful to get to share my debut Love Inspired Suspense story with you.

Tara and Tucker both struggle with the ability to trust. For Tucker, compound that with the guilt over the death of a fellow soldier and the certainty that God has abandoned him. It takes Tara and Tucker lowering their defenses in order to work together to stay alive and stay one step ahead of a killer bent on their destruction. Tara's deep faith and trust in God allow Him to move in their situation and reawaken the trust in God Tucker thought he'd buried for good.

God loves us so much, and when we lean into Him for wisdom and strength, He blesses us above anything we could hope for.

I love hearing from my readers. Please visit my website at ginabellauthor.com, or visit me on Facebook.

Blessings,
Gina

Get up to 4 Free Books!

We'll send you 2 free books from each series you try
PLUS a free Mystery Gift.

FREE Value Over **$25**

Both the **Love Inspired®** and **Love Inspired®** Suspense series feature compelling novels filled with inspirational romance, faith, forgiveness and hope.